The Man Called Teacher

By David A. Poulsen

Print ISBNs
BWL Print 9780228611554
Amazon Print 9780228611592
LSI Print 9780228611608

BWL Publishing Inc.

*Books we love to write ...
Authors around the world.*

http://bwlpublishing.ca

Dedication

To the memory of my father, Lawrence A. Poulsen (Larry) who loved the life of the cowboy, and to Wayne Lucas, who lived the life of the cowboy.

Acknowledgments

BWL Publishing Inc. acknowledges the Province of Alberta for their Provincial Operating Grant for Publishers, for its financial support,

Prologue

There's not much there now. They didn't rebuild the school after it burned down the second time. All you'd see, if you happened to go by the place, is the wood and stone cross Archie Cuddy made. I think he did a good job of it. It's pretty well understood that the cross is meant to honour only two of the people who died there and that it has nothing to do with the other five who also ended their lives that day. I don't know how I feel about that. It seems like even bad people ought to have a cross or something to remember them by.

Sometimes on a peaceful afternoon I still like to ride out there and sit and think about that day and the ones that led up to it.

Chapter One

It's because so many people have asked about it, and told me I should write it all down, that I finally decided to do this. Of course, it all took place almost four years ago now. I'm not sure I'll remember everything exactly the way it was, but between what gets set down here and what you already know about it, I expect the story will be mighty close to complete. When I think about it, I suppose I am the best one to tell it all right, just because I was there. Everyone else who was in the school during those four days in October of '96 is either dead or has gone away somewhere. My name, by the way, is William Dearing.

The thing that's hard is knowing just where to start. You'd probably think I should begin with Teacher himself, I mean the first time I saw him. But that wouldn't be right. Not exactly. Because if anybody should ever read this that isn't from around here, or never heard of the Kecking Horse School Trouble, they'd naturally have questions. Such as how it came about that somebody like me, a clerk in J. Harper Westover's General Store, should have been mixed up in the thing at all.

The Kecking Horse School Trouble — that's what the newspaper people called it when they wrote it up. I heard it even made the papers as far away as Denver and St. Louis, but I can't say for sure since I never saw the stories myself. I guess that's something I should explain right off — the thing about Kecking Horse. It's pretty obvious that the name should be Kicking Horse with an 'i'. But it's been this way for thirty years or so now and I don't know if it'll ever be changed.

The blame can be placed squarely on two Texans, one called L. B. Kirby and the other a man named Block. I never heard his first name. They were cowboys, pure and simple. They came up as part of the David Shirk cattle drive of 1871 that drove Texas Longhorn cattle from Fort Worth to the Owyhee Mountains in Idaho for the silver miners there. Then they must've tired of cowboy life and headed northeast until they stopped just about where I'm sitting as I write this. Kirby built a feed store and Block started a saloon, ran it out of a tent at first, then eventually put up a building. And that was the start of the town.

Of course, neither of those buildings are here anymore. Well, that's not entirely accurate; I guess a small piece of what was the feed store is now the storage part of Archie Cuddy's livery. The saloon, it burned down close to ten years ago. Kirby and Block had been gone for quite a while by then. Went down Oregon way and held up the stage right outside a stop called

Jesse Robinson's Store. They were caught and then strung up outside the courthouse at Crutcher's Crossing three months later.

But their big mistake — I grant you getting yourself hung constitutes a sizable error in itself — was saddling this community with a name that makes it look like we're all uneducated people. Shortly after those two Texans settled here and a few other folks joined them, Block decided the place needed a name. He figured Kicking Horse was appropriate since right at that moment, Kirby was laid up from being kicked square in the middle of the back by a stud horse named Bob.

So, Block rode off to the state legislature to get the name recorded. But don't forget, both men were Texans which means their version of spoken English wasn't like that of a lot of folks. When Block, who couldn't read or write any better than a poplar stump, pronounced the name for the government clerk fella, he said Kecking Horace. The clerk repeated it and Block said, "Yep, that's it. "

And that's how it was written down. It was just luck that another clerk came along and changed Horace to Horse, but I guess nobody noticed the Kecking part. Which, if you ask me, says something about government clerks and Texans. And we're still Kecking Horse to this day.

To return to the business of where and when I should start the story, I've thought long and hard about it, and to me, it makes sense to begin with Marcus Warren, who I guess was the closest thing to a Judge that there was around here at that time. He'd also got himself appointed as the Superintendent of Education or some such title. It was Mr. Warren (nobody called him Judge, not even when he was officiating over legal business) who came to me and asked if I'd be willing to put up the new teacher. My answer was to say I didn't know right off. He said I was the logical one since I lived in the nicest house in Kecking Horse and even though I was a bachelor, nobody would question the arrangement since my mother was under the same roof.

I said I still wasn't altogether sure about the thing, which is when he brought up the matter of the twelve dollars a month. The sum I'd be paid for having the teacher in my home. Then he made some jokes about how maybe I'd even lose my bachelorhood if the teacher was pretty enough. I didn't much care for those jokes, but I thought some more about that twelve dollars and figured the 'arrangement' — Mr. Warren called it that at least five times in the ten minutes we stood there talking — might not be so bad. Spending money was a little scarce back then, not that there was much to spend it on if you had some. I also felt having someone to talk to other than Mother, who mostly talked about religion, politics and the comings and goings of Nettie Whitman, might prove to be pleasurable.

So, I agreed, but not before I asked Mr. Warren why it was we were bringing in a teacher when we'd never had one before.

"Hell, it should be obvious," he told me, "there's more kids than there's ever been, most of 'em don't know much more than their letters if they know that much. Even our town's name is spelled wrong, that's how wanting the whole education issue has been around here."

And that was it. It was decided. There was going to be a teacher; an ad had been placed in some big city papers; Miss T. I. Morgan had answered the ad and soon would be living in my house. I started watching the Tuesday and Friday stagecoach arrivals from the front window of the store. It was a Friday in the late summer when the leaves had just started to turn and things were getting mighty busy in the store business, what with people getting ready for winter, that I received the first and second biggest surprises of my life. The stage was late that day (that wasn't one of the surprises; it was late most days) and there were only two people on it when it pulled in. One of them was our new school teacher. The other, I was to learn, was a man named Virgil Watts.

The new teacher was the first surprise. You might've guessed by now, if you didn't already know it, that T. I. Morgan wasn't a "Miss" at all. In fact, pretty far from it. He stood about a head taller than me which would put him about a couple or three inches over six feet tall. Looked like he'd spent a lot of time in the sun.

Not old, not young. He was a wide-set man, especially at the shoulders, and he was wearing a gun. Not exactly what I'd expected from someone who was going to be teaching letters and numbers and such to kids. Of course, at that point, I didn't know that was what he was here to do. He looked like somebody who might break horses for a living or punch cows or something. Or maybe have something to do with the law, on one side or the other, just the way he walked and looked around. The other surprise was the man, Virgil Watts. He was black, the first black man I'd ever seen, since very few Negro people ever got up into this part of the country, a fact that hasn't changed all that much right up to the present.

I stepped away from the window because I didn't want either of them to know I was watching them. When they walked into the store a few minutes later, I was trying to look like I was busy stacking some linens that had come in a week or so earlier.

"I'm Teacher." That was the first thing he said which is maybe why the name stuck the way it did. There were a few people in the store right then, and we talked about it afterwards. Everybody was pretty well agreed that he didn't say *the* teacher. Just Teacher. Like it was his name. And from then on, it was the only name I ever heard him called by, including by himself. Until right near the end, that is.

Once they were in the store, I had a chance to study on them a little further. Mostly I was staring at Teacher, all the time hoping it would look like I wasn't really interested at all. He had a face that whenever I try to describe it, I find I can't recall exact details. Oh, I can picture the simple things — tall man, big at the shoulder like I said, a lot of his clothes were black or at least dark, stuff like that. But the details are where I have trouble. You ever know someone like that?

Except I remember the wrinkles at the corners of his eyes, like he was somebody who laughed a lot. Which, of course, many of us were to find out later was absolutely factual. And he always looked like he needed a shave, even right after he'd had one. I didn't notice his clothes much, except the part about them being mostly dark, but I do recall his hat, I guess because I liked it and wished I had one like it. It was black too with a wide brim and just a bit of curve to it. Real nice hat.

"Yes, sir," is what I think I said in answer to his introduction.

"You are the gentleman who has a room for me?" Of course, when he said that, it occurred to me he was reporting for work as the school teacher for Kecking Horse District.

He looked around the store a little then which gave me a bit of time to work on my reply.

Not *enough* time though, which is why I just said "uh..."

He smiled then, not a big smile but friendly enough. "Maybe I'm not quite what you expected"

"Uh ... no, sir, not ... exactly."

"But you do have a place for me to stay."

Since it wasn't actually a question, I didn't have to think as hard about my answer. I nodded.

"Good," he said. "This is my friend, Virgil Watts," he gestured in the direction of the black man who had taken off his hat when he'd entered the store. "We'd be obliged if you happened to have a room for him as well. He won't be staying long since he'll be catching on with one of the local ranches within a few days, but in the meantime ..."

I was wishing Mr. Warren would just drop into the store right then as he often did, but those things never happen when you want them to. I was sure he would be quick to tell this man that his services wouldn't be required, and while he was at it, he could also inform Mr. Virgil Watts that there wasn't likely to be work on any of the ranches around Kecking Horse for a black cowboy.

Since Mr. Warren wasn't present, and wasn't likely to be present in the next thirty seconds or so, which is about as long as I figured I could reasonably hold off on saying something, I had a feeling that whatever it was I said could have some considerable impact on the immediate future of our community. Of course, I had no way of knowing at that moment just how considerable that impact was to be. Or maybe things would have happened the way they did no matter what came out of my mouth just then. Anyway, I shrugged and said, "I'm sure Mother and I can find a place for Mr. Watts."

As I recall, I was looking at the gun in Teacher's holster as I said it. It was a .44 caliber Smith and Wesson I found out later. It had a different look to it, the barrel and all, and the holster it sat in was tied around his leg. I seemed to have a recollection that a holster tied like that was the mark of a gunfighter, but I wasn't about to ask about that. And I noticed the inside of the holster looked like it had been covered in some kind of animal fur — rabbit or some such I guessed, which I had an idea was the sort of thing a man would want if he needed his gun to leave its holster kind of quick and smooth. Something else we found out later was that that gun had taken at least four men's lives…twice that many if you believe Cooper Raine's ravings, which not many of us do.

"I ... I can't leave the store just now to take you there," I hoped they wouldn't offer to make their way on their own. I figured an unexpected visit from one man with a gun, and one who was not white, might provide the kind of shock to Mother's nervous system that could shorten her life considerably.

"Fine," Teacher said, "we'll just wander across the street to see if the livery has anything in the way of horses we might be able to afford.

You'll find us in the saloon when you close up shop."

"There isn't one," I said.

"No livery? I thought we saw one just down the street as the stage was coming in."

"Yes, sir. We have a livery. There's no saloon."

"No saloon?" Teacher looked surprised. A lot of people are when they hear that. "Where do folks refresh themselves?"

"There's a small bar at the hotel. It isn't much more than a big room," I said.

"That's where we'll be."

I found them there later. Which, in itself, was another surprise. I never figured Jake Drury would allow a black man on the premises of the Independent Cities Hotel Bar, let alone serve him. But when I walked in, the two newcomers were leaning on the bar, each with a glass in his hand, and it looked like they were talking, though if they were, you couldn't hear it because they were speaking so softly. Jake Drury didn't look happy about the whole thing, but I figured he must have got a look at the .44 and decided against making an issue of it. I walked over to where Teacher and Virgil Watts were standing.

"Drink?" Teacher looked at me.

"No thanks. I just came to see if you wanted to have a look at your rooms." I didn't bother to tell them that I'd stopped by the house after I closed up the store. I'd thought it best to prepare Mother for our guests. She took it better than I thought she would.

"Are they clean?" was all she said.

I told her they were, even though, to tell the truth, the state of their cleanliness wasn't something I had paid much attention to when Teacher and Watts walked into the store.

Teacher nodded and swallowed the last of his drink.

"Ready?" he asked Virgil Watts.

"Uh-huh," Watts said.

Thirty seconds. That's all it would have taken. If I'd got there thirty seconds earlier, we'd have been on our way to Mother's roast of beef dinner and berry pie and Teacher's first day in Kecking Horse would have passed without incident. But that isn't at all the way things went. As we were starting for the door of the bar, it opened and in walked Joad Cook, Marty Waincastle and a man I didn't know. The first two were hands from the Bar U, a big spread up in the Canadian territories, which is just a couple days' ride north of here. The Bar U starts just over the border and stretches north a long way, almost to Calgary. I figured the third man must be a new rider for the same outfit. He was kind of in the shadows and I didn't get a real good look at him. Besides, most of my attention was on the other two.

A lot of the men from the Bar U came to the Independent Cities Hotel to drink when they had time off or when they were doing business around here. Still do, as a matter of fact. Most of them are all right. Cook and Waincastle weren't. Especially Waincastle. He got in a lot of fights and didn't pay his gambling debts, which started even more fights. One day he shot Cooper Raine's favourite mule after he stepped in one of the mule's plops, which since it was in the street, could hardly be blamed on the mule.

It was the only time in my life I'd ever felt sorry for Cooper Raine who is a hard man to feel sorry for because he has a voice like a magpie and is a liar to boot. Still, when I saw him kneeling in the dust alongside that dying mule which turned out to be his favourite, and there were tears on his face and for once he wasn't talking, I felt pretty bad for Cooper.

When I saw those three come into the bar, I had an uncomfortable feeling. I started to get awful warm which is how I usually get when there's unpleasantness in the air. I don't think Teacher or Watts took any notice of the three, other than to see them come in, and were about to step around them and continue on out the door.

"For Chrissake, Jake," Joad Cook said real loud. "For Chrissake," he said again, "what has become of your drinking establishment? Surely this isn't a nigger I see?"

The arrival of the other men must have helped Jake Drury find his courage. "Yeah, it's a Goddamn nigger all right, but he's on his way out and he better not be thinkin' about comin' back."

By that time my stomach was so upset I had pretty well lost all interest in Mother's roast of beef dinner, and I was starting to think a little about how my obituary would read if there'd actually been a paper in town. One thing I did know was that Jake kept a shotgun behind the bar and I could also see all three of the new arrivals were well armed.

I took a couple of steps to one side and to my surprise, Teacher and Virgil Watts followed me. They stepped around Marty Waincastle who was on the outside of the three, and we walked out of the bar. My stomach started to settle as soon as we got outside. The sun was dropping behind the buildings on the west side of the street. I wanted to look over at Teacher and Watts, but decided not to, my thinking being that humiliation isn't really humiliation until somebody calls attention to it. It didn't matter though, because we weren't even a decent rock throw from the bar when we heard the doors open and swing shut behind us. This time it was Waincastle who spoke.

"You girls planning to be in town for a while?"

We kept walking. I could hear them come up close behind us.

"I'm talking to you, lady," Waincastle grabbed Teacher's arm and swung him around. Watts and I turned around, too.

"You must be mistaken," Teacher said. "There are no ladies in this street. Just us three men and you three boys."

As soon as he said the word *boys*, my mind started working on the obituary again.

"Ooh, now will you listen to that?" Cook's laugh was more of a cackle than anything. "You as tough as you talk?"

Just then Cook, who'd brought a bottle out of the bar with him, took a drink. He was lowering the bottle when Teacher hit him. Three times. Twice with his left hand and once with his right.

Back when I was a kid and I was off by myself, fishing or something, I'd sometimes have these daydreams. In one of them I'm walking along with a pretty woman and some bad man — he was real big in every one of those daydreams — would step up and insult her and I'd break his nose with one punch. Except in the daydream the man's nose didn't make any noise as it was breaking. There was lots of blood, of course, but it all happened in silence. I realize now those daydreams were missing something in the accuracy department. A man's nose makes a very definite sound as it breaks. It's something like the crunch you get when you step on a June bug, except with a breaking nose, there's more of a pulpy, drawn-out effect to the crunch.

Cook dropped the bottle and went down to his knees with both hands on his face as if he was trying to keep the blood from getting out. And squealing, he was doing a lot of squealing. Teacher turned to Waincastle just as the cowboy was swinging his own bottle at Teacher's head.

Teacher ducked just enough to make the bottle glance of his shoulder. Then he came up and hit Waincastle with a backhand that lifted the cowboy right off the ground and dropped him flat on his back.

But Waincastle was a tough hombre, you remember I mentioned that, and from flat on the ground he reached down and got his hand on his gun and was about to pull it. Teacher took one step and kicked Waincastle between the legs as hard as I've ever seen anybody kick man or beast. Waincastle's hand fell away from his gun and he rolled over on his side, groaning and puking up at the same time.

Things had been happening fast and I'd kind of lost track of Watts and the other man who'd come into the bar with Cook and Waincastle. I looked now in their direction; the man I didn't know was leaning against a post and neither he nor Watts had moved. I was glad to see that. What I wasn't so glad to see was that Jake Drury was standing on the step in front of the Independent Cities Hotel Bar with his shotgun. He had it aimed right at Teacher. They stood for a few seconds looking at each other. Then the third cowboy, the one who was with Cook and Waincastle, straightened up kind of lazy-like and spoke. It was the first words I'd heard him say and he was talking to Jake.

"Now, Bartender, it seems to me you've got a decision to make," he spoke real slow, like he had all the time in the world. "You've got to decide whether, in the fifth of a second it'll take the buckshot to get from the barrel of your gun to that man's belly, he can get his gun out and get off a shot. Turns out I know this fella and I'd be betting that he can. If it turns out I'm right, you have another decision to make and that's whether these two daisies who are busy making a mess of your street are worth dying for." He stopped then and stared at Jake who was still watching Teacher. It was only a few seconds of silence that kind of hung there but it seemed a lot longer. I imagine it must have seemed like a month or so to Jake Drury who seemed to be feeling the effects of the heat in much the same way I was.

"I can see you're having a little trouble deciding," the cowboy said with a little smile on his face that I doubt I'll ever forget, "so let's see if I can help you. Let's just say I'm wrong and this man doesn't get off that shot and kill you like I'm betting he will, well, if that doesn't happen, then I'll kill you myself. Does that help you at all in making up your mind?"

Jake looked over at the cowboy who was still smiling that little smile. "You sayin' you like niggers and nigger lovers, mister?"

"I like 'em a lot better than fat-ass bartenders with shotguns," the cowboy said.

Jake blinked and then he looked back at Teacher and slowly, very slowly, he lowered the shotgun, backed up a couple of steps, turned and went back inside.

Cook and Waincastle were both still making noises that weren't pleasing to listen to. Teacher turned to the cowboy I didn't know.

"Harry." He nodded. "Sorry I didn't greet you inside, but I didn't recognize you. It's a little dark in there."

The man named Harry nodded, but that was all.

"What brings you this far north?" Teacher asked.

"Breaking some horses at the Bar U, up on the Highwood," Harry told him. "Probably stay around for the winter. Got me a half share in a hotel up in Calgary."

"Hope it's a little more hospitable than this place." Teacher grinned.

"Stop by you're ever up that way," Harry's small smile was back in place.

"I will. Seen Butch lately?"

"He's in Wyoming. What about yourself?"

"Teaching school," Teacher said.

The man called Harry didn't seem at all surprised that a man who had just whipped two of the local toughs and stared down a shotgun was our school teacher. But then he didn't look like someone who would be surprised by much.

"So long, Harry," Teacher said.

Harry nodded again as he bent down to help Cook to his feet.

We turned and walked away then. Teacher hadn't introduced us around which was to be expected. I'd learned a long time before that the people who rode in and out of towns like

Kecking Horse preferred to remain pretty close to anonymous. That's why first names or nicknames were often all you heard. It was some time later that I found out who Harry — turns out his last name was Longabaugh — and his friend Butch Cassidy were. Of course, by then, pretty well everybody knew about them.

I looked over at Teacher. The scuffle didn't seem to have ruffled his clothes or soiled him at all. He was as clean as if he'd spent the last hour in church. Mother would be much relieved.

Chapter Two

People laugh at me sometimes. At least they used to before the Kecking Horse School Trouble. They don't as much anymore. I guess being part of something that turns out to be famous like that earns you a certain amount of respect. I didn't really do much; at least I don't view my own part in it as very much, even if I did kill a man before it was all over.

I'd never been in a fight; in fact, I'd never even owned a gun before what happened at the school. Most of the time I prefer to read books, which a lot of folks in this part of the country see as a wasteful way to spend your time. So, people made fun of me and I can't say I liked it at all.

There isn't much of me to look at, and what there is, wouldn't be what you'd call handsome in any way. I'm a little on the scrawny side and my face has too many sharp corners to it to be what women would find striking. Some years back, I tried to grow a moustache, but it didn't take. My hair is light-coloured and my face is lighter still. Mostly I'd describe me as ordinary. And maybe respectable in appearance.

I do have one talent that's considered useful on the frontier. Turns out I'm good with horses. I guess it's because my pa, when he was still alive, always had horses around and since I was never more than a step and a half away from his side as I was growing up, I got used to working with them. I don't want to sound boastful (and anyway, it has something to do with the story I'm telling), but people used to bring their bronkiest colts out to our place for my pa and me to break. And after a while I think I was almost as good at it as he was.

Of course, that was back in the days when we lived out by Medicine Creek at the edge of the hills to the west of here. It wasn't until Pa was killed that Mother and I moved to town. And I guess what people kept saying after that was right. I probably did become sort of a 'Mama's boy' — that's what they called me — since I didn't have a wife and mostly read books and worked as a store clerk and all. Still, every once in a while, even now, someone will bring me a horse nobody can ride and even though I'm not around horses all the time like I was when I was growing up, I can still usually get by a bad one. I guess it's just one of those abilities some people have or inherit or something.

Maybe that's why people still talk about the way Pa was killed. He was dragged home one day eight years before the school trouble, one foot still in the stirrup. Naturally people figured he got thrown when the horse spooked, and he died from the dragging. That's how his body looked, that's for sure. It was pretty terrible for Mother and me when that horse came into the yard with Pa hanging out the side, all bloody and broken up.

Mother was never the same person after that. We moved into town and you could count on the fingers of one hand the number of times she went outside of the house in the years that followed. People thought of her as old, even I did, but the truth is she was some years from fifty when Teacher arrived in Kecking Horse.

I guess, Pa getting killed that way probably changed me some, too. For one thing, I became suspicious of things and people in a way I'd never been before. I don't know that I ever really believed Pa had been drug to death by that horse. First of all, she was his favourite mare, a feisty thing but a horse I would've thought could be trusted. I always had this feeling that maybe Pa had come across something he wasn't supposed to see out there in the hills — there'd always been whispers, still are, in fact, of things going on out there that most folks either don't know about or don't talk about. It felt like to me that it was made to look like the horse killed him.

Anyway, I told you I'd get around to what all this horse stuff has to do with Teacher and Virgil Watts. You remember, they'd gone off to the livery when they left the store that first day. Well, it turns out they bought a couple of horses all right. Or perhaps, it would be more accurate to say they came to own two horses. They only *bought* one, the other horse was thrown in on the deal.

The horse they purchased, a paint, was owned by Archie Cuddy who runs the livery. The other horse was his too. It was a horse that had been running alone in a pasture outside of town. Nobody had laid a hand on him in three years. At least Archie said it was three. My own feeling is that nobody had *ever* touched the horse since he was full grown. I'd told Archie a couple of summers earlier I'd break him for fourteen dollars (my regular price was ten) but I guess Archie figured it wouldn't say much for his own abilities as a horseman if he hired me. So, the horse just stayed out there. Alone and wild and full of hate. He was a big black gelding that thought he was still a stud. Except there were no mares around which, of course, is frustrating for a stud or even a gelding who thinks he's one. Archie called him Prince, which I suppose was Archie's way of being funny.

That first night, after the fight in the street, we were having dinner when Teacher told me he'd bought a paint horse from Archie and the liveryman threw in a horse named Prince. I almost choked on Mother's roast of beef when I heard that.

When I recovered, I said, "He's not a real good horse," not wanting to overstate the situation.

"I figured he probably wasn't," Teacher nodded as he loaded more mashed potatoes onto his plate. "Anytime somebody gives you a horse, you can count on it being the next thing to a killer."

I looked over at Mother when Teacher said the word 'killer' but she was concentrating, or pretending to, on a slice of the roast of beef.

"If you need any help with him, I have Saturday afternoon off and I could come and give you a hand," I said.

Teacher didn't look at me funny like a lot of people would if someone like me offered to help break a horse.

"Thanks," he said. "If the horse was for me, I'd take you up on that. Turns out he belongs to Virgil here, and he's pretty handy with broncs."

I studied on Virgil Watts for the first time. He wasn't real big but he looked solid enough. He was as broad through the chest as Teacher was, which made him appear impressive due to the fact he was a few inches shorter. The look on his face was intense but not angry, you know, like it is with some people. His eyes were open wide and gave the impression at first that he was staring, but if you looked at him for a while, you came to see him as somebody who was just real interested in watching the world go on around him. I decided right then that Teacher was probably right. Watts looked like he could probably handle a bad horse if he had to. And any other bad stuff that happened along, too.

As I mentioned before, he was pretty well my first experience around a black man, and I didn't know if that way he had of looking out at the world was the way all black people regarded life, or if it was a singular characteristic of Virgil Watts. As I write this four years later, I still haven't figured that out.

The following Saturday was one of the best days of my life. Teacher and Watts invited me to ride out to the pasture where Archie Cuddy kept Prince so's I could witness that first meeting of horse and man. On the way out there, Watts rode double behind me and carried his saddle, his reasoning being he'd have a horse to ride on the way back. And he talked. I found out Watts, who didn't often say a whole bunch, became plumb chatty when it came to the subject of horses. In fact, he had a complete philosophy he'd developed on the subject of understanding the horse mentality, a philosophy he'd share with anybody who'd listen.

"First of all," he said in a kind of drawly dialect that I can't duplicate, so I won't try, "the rider's got to be smarter than the horse. If the horse gits to thinkin' he's the smarter one, he ain't about to respect the person on his back and that can make for trouble."

That made sense to me since Archie Cuddy had had nothing but trouble with this horse and I've always felt that a horse, or any other creature, would have to be awfully dull witted to out-stupid Archie.

"Now, once the horse feels respect for the rider, from then on it's a matter of makin' every move feel as natural as a bird zippin' around in a tree. That way the horse gets to feelin' that the saddle, and the man in it and the bit in his mouth, are as much a part of him as his withers or his hocks, see?"

I saw and even agreed, but I still wasn't convinced that all of this logic was going to work with Prince. I listened to Watts's theories of horse psychology most of the way out to the pasture.

The other thing that was interesting about the ride was Teacher. He didn't pay any attention at all to the conversation or the countryside or anything else. He was reading a book as he rode along. I'd never actually seen anybody do that before, but the thing is he didn't look as strange as you might think. And I doubt that anybody would have called him any of the things they call me when I read books. I expect the .44 on his right hip probably would have discouraged any loose talk of that kind. I have to admit he presented a different image of a reader than I do with the thick glasses I have to wear to read and, of course, no .44.

"What's he reading?" I whispered to Watts when we were about halfway to our destination.

"B'lieve it's called Withering Heat," he whispered back, "ya know it?"

"Sure," I nodded sagely, "know it well. Read it a couple of times. It's a story about some people in a desert."

Watts nodded back and smiled. "That's what I figured."

I was never sure if he knew I was fibbing or not. Truth is, I did read the book a year or so later, in fact, the very copy Teacher was holding in his hand. I've read that book and most of the others by the Bronte sisters since then, and none of them, as you probably know, is about people in a desert.

We got to the pasture — Archie had built a makeshift sort of fence to keep Prince from leaving the country altogether — and for several minutes the three of us sat there sizing up the black horse. Archie had diverted a bit off the creek that flowed through that piece of land so it trickled through Prince's pasture. Meaning, except for the lack of companionship with other horses, Prince was reasonably comfortable.

Prince watched us ride in. He stayed a comfortable distance on the other side of the fence and appeared to be doing some sizing up of his own.

After a considerable period of time had gone by, Teacher looked at Watts and then at me. "I vote we ride back to town and buy another horse."

Had it come to a vote, I would have been tempted to cast mine with Teacher. I won't go so far as to say Prince frightened me, but it was becoming clear he wasn't happy to see us and would do everything he could to make our Saturday unpleasant. Since our arrival, he had not stopped pawing, snorting and rearing. These are generally considered to be fairly strong indications a horse may have a difficult side to him. But what made Prince stand out from the average bad horse was the fact that as he was doing those things, he was also backing around in tight circles. Then when his back was completely to us, he would kick out, as hard and as fast as I've ever seen a horse kick. Now, no horse I've ever come across is dumb enough to think that he's going to be able to kick anybody who's a hundred yards off. So, I guessed that the backing and kicking was his way of warning us.

Watts seemed not to notice. He slid off the back of my horse and set his saddle down. "I don't plan to ride double back to town," he said.

"By the look of that black horse out there," Teacher said, "I'd say you've got two options. You either ride double or you walk." He was obviously enjoying the whole thing, which I thought might have had something to do with the fact he wasn't the one who would be getting on Prince.

Watts turned to me." "You any good with a rope?"

"Not much," I admitted.

"Then may I borrow your horse? I don't think there's much chance of any of us walking up to that horse and slipping a halter on him."

I stepped off my horse. "His name's Powder," I said, though I can't say why I felt Watts was in need of that particular piece of information.

And Watts, after first uncoiling, then recoiling one of several lariats he had brought along, stepped up into the saddle. I walked over and opened the gate to let him into the pasture. As he rode slowly by me and into the field that until now had been the sole property of Prince, I could hear him speaking softly, apparently to himself.

"Respect, that's all. Got to get his respect. Got to let him know I'm smarter than he is. Then, once we understand each other ..."

I didn't hear the rest because he got out of hearing range. He crossed the diverted creek that went through one corner of the field and moved closer to the horse on the other side. Meanwhile, Prince was continuing to snort, paw, kick and make other inhospitable gestures. He had moved about two-thirds of the way down to the other end of the pasture and the only time he took his eyes off us was during the kicking-out-behind part of his ritual.

Watts walked my horse slowly across the pasture toward the angry black animal that had shown no sign of changing the way he felt about us. I admit I was a little concerned about Powder who I was quite certain had never encountered a horse quite like Prince, but he seemed to be handling things reasonably well, at least so far. I could hear Watt's voice again. He'd increased his volume a little, I assumed because he wanted Prince to hear. I could tell he was trying to soothe and quiet the horse although I couldn't make out the words themselves.

Unfortunately for Watts, the horse was neither soothed nor quiet. Several times, just as Watts got close enough to swing his rope, Prince snorted and moved out of range. It looked to me like the thing had become a game, at least as far as Prince was concerned. And it appeared he knew how to play it quite well.

I was to learn something about Virgil Watts during those hours on that hot afternoon. I was to learn that he was a man of Biblical patience. I'm guessing an hour or more passed before he actually got to throw his rope. I'm not sure whether Prince finally became bored or if he got careless after all that time.

Anyway, Watts swung, threw and caught. I was impressed that his arm had been perfectly true with his first throw. Sadly, that was the only impressive thing about that first catch, although I'm willing to accept at least some of the blame for what happened next. After all, he was riding my horse and he was in my saddle. So, I suppose it should have fallen to me to check my cinch. Although Teacher said later, after he'd stopped laughing, that it's a cowboy's responsibility to check his own cinch before he throws his rope. The thing is, I didn't, and Watts didn't.

As a result, when Prince threw the fit all of us expected he would, Virgil Watts and my saddle were immediately jerked down and to the right, I'd say about ninety degrees worth. Watts, as I've said, was a very good cowboy and maybe the second best man in the saddle I've ever seen, after my Pa, so I can testify quite honestly that for several seconds he and the saddle remained together despite the fact both were sticking straight out from the right side of my horse. I believe I also mentioned that Powder was very well broke. However, he was not so well broke that he was willing to tolerate a riding style he was completely unfamiliar with.

He began to buck. Not little bitty crow hops but head-down, bowed-back, reach for the sky stuff, about one buck per second, I'd guess. And Watts, already awkwardly positioned to the starboard side of Powder's body, finally fell off. The saddle followed, once the cinch snapped, which didn't take long. Now, a new problem presented itself. The loop end of the rope was still around Prince's neck. The other end was securely fastened to my saddle horn.

Dragging a wildly bouncing saddle over the prairie seemed to upset Prince and he no longer snorted and trotted. Now he raced around and around the pasture, every once in a while, jumping high in the air almost as if he were trying to jump something. The faster he went, the crazier the movements of the trailing saddle became. Several times it bounced to heights several feet off the ground. To complete the picture, you have to be able to see my horse, Powder, bucking in a smaller circle inside the large circle Prince was tracing and retracing with his laps around the pasture.

It was at that moment I heard Virgil Watts say, "Shit." That was the only time I ever heard him utter that or any other off-colour word. And, to tell you the truth, though Mother would disapprove of my saying so, I couldn't blame him then, or even now, as I reflect back on it.

Eventually, the saddle lodged itself against a fencepost and the rope snapped, leaving the saddle on the ground while Prince, free of the annoying object, continued his course around the outer perimeter of the pasture for two more, somewhat slower, circuits. Powder wore himself out and stopped in the middle of the field. Stillness and a kind of calm took possession of the pasture, but it was the kind of calm that I always figured must fall over a battlefield between phases of a battle. Watts walked over to where his saddle was but before he picked it up, he stopped, turned slightly away from us and began to relieve himself. I modestly turned completely around to look at Teacher and to my surprise he was doing the same thing.

I'm ashamed to say what I'm about to, but I promised myself when I started this chronicle that I'd record every detail as faithfully and with as much historical accuracy as possible, so I'll tell it anyway. As I watched the two men simultaneously making water, it occurred to me that perhaps there was some ritual attached to the taming of particularly wild horses that collective pissing was a part of. So, I figured the least I could do to help this day end on a positive note was to participate in the ritual. I turned in a new direction and urinated. For the next couple of minutes, the only sound was three jets of water striking the prairie soil. As I said, I feel foolish even mentioning it now.

In any event, we finished, rearranged ourselves and Watts went on with the business of capturing and taking control of Prince. He moved away from his saddle, retrieved mine, made some repairs to the mangled cinch, re-saddled Powder and with a second lariat set off once more after his prize. I walked back to where Teacher was alternating between reading his novel and laughing. I'm quite certain his laughing had nothing to do with the contents of the book. He made no attempt to contain the volume of his laughter as I had done during some of the day's more entertaining moments. If Watts noticed, he gave no indication, although as Teacher and I looked out at him now, we could see his lips moving. He was clearly conversing again with Prince.

"I'll bet he's not saying the same things to that horse that I would be," Teacher grinned at me, "Virgil's more polite than I am."

"Do you think he'll give up?" I was thinking back to my pa's attitude toward horses. He was the most patient man I'd ever known with animals and I'm not sure he'd have wanted to ride Prince bad enough to go through what Watts had so far that afternoon. And Watts was no closer to breaking the horse than when he'd started.

Teacher looked at Watts and squinted against the sun, "He'll starve to death, and us with him, before he goes home without that horse."

I thought about that. A picture formed in my mind of the three of us, our remains being found by some future traveler, who would first notice a large black horse — healthy and snorty as a colt, a length of sun-baked, tattered lariat dangling from his neck — walking over and around our bones. I took a renewed interest in what was happening in that pasture, and the next three times Watts threw his rope and missed, I didn't laugh. As a matter of fact, Watts never did catch the horse again; what he did, however, was get close enough to pick up the frayed end of the first rope he'd thrown that was still attached to Prince's bulky neck. He managed to get it dallied around his saddle horn. That's when Prince took up the plunging and crazy running that worked so well for him the first time. This time the cinch held, as did the rope, and for several minutes Watts played the black horse like a fish, first letting him run, then dallying a little tighter. Each wrap of the dally brought Prince and Virgil Watts closer together.

Finally, they stood side by side, both breathing heavily and nearly exhausted. But as I looked at them, I had the feeling they both knew the most important part of the struggle was still to come. Watts was still talking, very softly now and occasionally he'd reach out a hand to touch Prince's mane. From the horse's reaction, it was obvious no human hand had touched him in a very long time, and he didn't like the idea of it happening now.

Watts waved us over. He needed our help. Teacher and I walked out into the pasture where Watts was holding fast to Prince. He got down from my horse, pointed at me and I climbed back up into the saddle, taking a good hold on the rope dallied around the saddlehorn.

Watts wasn't saying much now. He looked grimmer than when we'd started and more tired and a lot more dirty. Teacher was still smiling. Watts took another rope, made a loop in one end, then passed it gently over Prince's back and after several tries managed to get Prince to step a front foot into the loop. Once the foot was caught, Watts gave it a good pull and Prince was forced to bring the foot into the air. Watts passed the rope to Teacher whose job it was to make sure the foot *stayed* in the air. We now had control of Prince's head and one front foot, the theory being that he would be as helpless as a newborn baby as Watts saddled him.

Prince had other ideas and there were several minutes of rearing and hopping on three legs before he finally, most likely from exhaustion, decided to stand still. Watts worked fast. There was no telling how long the calm spell would last. He laid the saddle on the horse's broad back and quickly reached under his belly to take hold of the cinch strap.

Prince tried to turn his head in the direction of Watts' nearest arm. Luckily, I had dallied Prince short enough that the horse's teeth stopped a few inches short of the fleshy part of Watts' exposed left arm. Watts did up the cinch and then surprised all of us by slipping a bridle over the immense black head before Prince seemed to figure out what was happening.

I thought Watts might want to rest for a few minutes before attempting that first ride but I was wrong. He leaped into the saddle and screamed "Yah!" so quickly and loudly that I forgot the ride couldn't start until I undallied the rope. Teacher was also caught by surprise and was still clutching the rope that held Prince's front foot in the air. What this meant, was that the horse's first moves were little straight up and down hops by a three-legged horse that Mother would have had a pretty good chance to ride through.

"Men," Watts said quietly, "if you don't let go of the ropes, it will not be possible for me to go someplace."

I could see he had a point and loosened the dally and was able to flip my rope over and off of Prince's head. It was a second or two before Prince realized he was free. In that second, Teacher tried to loosen the second rope enough to let it fall from the horse's front leg. Unfortunately for Watts, Teacher was a bit slow or maybe just unlucky. In any event, the loop remained attached to the horse's front foot with the end Teacher had been holding hanging out behind.

Prince blew and began a series of buck-jumps that covered a lot of ground in a short time. I'm convinced Watts would have been able to ride the horse through this period had not the free end of the rope that was attached to Prince's front foot flipped up and wrapped itself, with snake-like accuracy, around the rider's neck. Watts realized immediately if the situation remained unchanged — by that I mean if the rope were to remain where it was — he would soon be strangled to death. Each time the horse bucked his front foot shot a little further away from the other end of the rope that was coiled around Watts's neck. That meant the neck end of the rope was getting tighter.

Watts let go of the reins and saddle and with both hands free was able to get the rope off his neck at almost the exact second he was thrown out of the saddle and to the ground.

Watts lay on the ground for quite a while watching Prince continue his tour of the pasture. I think he realized that if he hadn't got the rope off his neck when he did, he might not have disengaged it at all. That would have meant being dragged behind Prince and very likely being killed, especially if it were up to Teacher and me to get him freed.

I looked over at Teacher. He was down on one knee in a prayer-like position, his head down. Except he wasn't praying. He was laughing. In fact, as I looked more closely, I noticed that he was laughing so hard that there were tears on his cheeks and some of them were falling into the dry pasture dust. It was quite some time before either of those two men were able to speak, although for very different reasons.

Several minutes later, it was Virgil Watts who broke the silence. Even with all the excitement, he still spoke in a soft voice as he addressed Teacher. "That might have worked out better if you'd got that rope off his leg," was all he said.

Teacher nodded and looked serious, maybe even a little guilty, but I had the feeling he was having to work rather hard at it. Eventually, Watts caught Prince again; we got him dallied up and tightened up the saddle. This time Watts removed the rope from Prince's leg before he mounted up. Once in the saddle, he directed Teacher to open the gate at the end of the pasture.

I released the horse again and watched as the two of them toured the pasture a couple of times, Prince leaping and diving, whirling and sun fishing, Watts sitting in the saddle like he was riding a plough horse to church. Eventually, Prince spotted the open gate, pinned his ears back, and went through it at a rate of speed I've not often seen. In a few seconds Prince and Watts disappeared around a hill, leaving only a settling trail of dust behind them. I looked over at Teacher. He was putting his book in his saddlebag.

"Well, that's it," he said." Might as well head for town. Our work's done."

"Hadn't we better follow them?"

"No need." Teacher shook his head.

"What if he gets throwed?"

"He won't. They'll be back to town long before us and when they get there, Virgil will have himself a broke horse."

Teacher was right, by the way.

Now I know there will be those who will question the need to tell the episode about Prince and Watts and the way Teacher laughed about it all, but I wanted to put it down for a reason. I could try to tell you they were just ordinary men who liked doing ordinary things and I know you wouldn't believe me. But that was what was most interesting about the man we called Teacher. He wasn't like any of the gunfighters I'd read about in the dime novels (I'd read plenty of them, I admit) you know, tough men who never smiled and never talked and only seemed to pass the time between killing folks by looking hard and cruel and smoking cigarettes and drinking whiskey. He was just a man who loved to laugh and to live. I think that's what makes what happened at Kecking Horse School all the more ... I don't know ... memorable.

Of course, Prince is an important part of the story for another reason, but I'll get to that before long. Two days later, Watts got a job cowboyin' up at the 40 Ranch, which was another surprise to a lot of us, him being black and all, but maybe word got around about how he'd been able to handle Prince and any man, black or white, who could do that was obviously a mighty good hand. Anyway, it was a Monday I think, that Virgil Watts and his newly broke horse rode out of town.

Chapter Three

Mr. Warren didn't like Teacher, right from the start. The first time they met was right there in the store and it wasn't friendly, not at all.

"About the best thing you can do for yourself is to get on the next available stage out of here, "Mr. Warren said. "We won't be having someone of your ilk teaching whatever it is you teach to our kids."

Teacher didn't say anything, so Mr. Warren went on. "As a matter of fact, you can consider yourself fortunate I don't have you charged with representing yourself in a fraudulent manner and let the law, of which I am a possessor of vested authority, deal with this appalling matter."

Up to then Teacher hadn't looked too interested in what Mr. Warren had to say. He'd been leaning on the glass case where we keep the men's shaving materials. He'd told me when he came in that he was looking to buy a new mug and brush and I'd directed him to the glass case. That's where Mr. Warren started in on him before I even had a chance to make a formal introduction.

I'd said, "Uh, this is ... Mr. Warren..." and that's as far as I got. Teacher held out his hand in greeting but Mr. Warren didn't shake it. He just started going on about Teacher getting out of town.

Eventually, Teacher straightened up and for once the smile was gone. He was a lot taller and a lot wider than Mr. Warren. "Just what is it in the way I've represented myself that you take exception to?" If I hadn't been standing right there at that counter, almost right next to Teacher, I doubt I'd have heard a word of what he said, that's how quiet he spoke to Mr. Warren.

"Well ... for one thing, you're not a woman. "Mr. Warren's voice wasn't quiet at all. "You know perfectly well that we wanted to hire a woman teacher. Our ad was clear and —"

"As a matter of fact, I *don't* know that, Mr. Warren." Teacher shook his head and reached in his jacket pocket. "I happen to have a copy of the ad with me and as I look at it, I see no reference at all to the fact that applicants were required to be female."

"But it's painfully obvious ... there's never been ... and anyway ..."

Teacher passed me the clipping, something I immediately wished he hadn't done.

"Would you mind reading that aloud and maybe we'll all see how clear the ad is, and, by the way, I agree that it is very clear."

I took the clipping and unfolded it and looked up at Mr. Warren and Teacher before I started reading. "Uh ..." I began. I start a lot of things that way. I guess it's sort of a nervous

42

habit. I was definitely nervous right then as I
read…

"There, you see?" Mr. Warren interrupted
me. "It's all right there. Unmarried, clean-living.
And that other stuff ... it's clear that we ..."

"Surely, Mr. Warren, you are not
suggesting that a *man* cannot be clean-living.
Why a look at yourself would certainly remove
all doubt on that point and as for unmarried ..."
Here, Teacher turned his head to look at me. His
smile was back, and I could see he was
beginning to enjoy himself.

"But, it's assumed that a teacher will be a
woman ..."

"Not by me," Teacher shook his head again.
I noticed little drops of perspiration had begun
to form on Mr. Warren's forehead. "Nor by the
schools I listed in my letter as references which
I'm sure you checked with before issuing me a
contract. Now, as for that contract, I'm sure a
man with your vested legal authority is well
aware that it is a binding, legal document and I
want you to understand that I will take the
appropriate steps if you decide you'd rather not
live up to your part of our agreement. I'll take

the white one and that brush with the red handle." That last part was addressed to me as he pointed at one of the mugs in the glass case.

"But I've sent for another teacher. A proper one. A woman. I did that as soon as I learned of this dreadful ... mistake." The drops on Mr. Warren's forehead had spread to his whole face and were beginning to roll down and drop onto his shirt, which extended out quite a ways so as to provide cover for his stomach.

"Mr. Warren," Teacher said as I handed him the mug and brush, "it sounds to me like you have a problem. But I'm not it. School starts next Monday, and I'll be there in front of the class when it does. You're welcome to stop by anytime and see how the lessons are going. Good day, Mr. Warren." Teacher handed me the money to pay for the shaving supplies and headed for the door.

Mr. Warren watched him go and then turned to look at me. He took a handkerchief out of his pocket and patted his head several times. Then, for the second time in a few days I was surprised by the next word that came from someone's lips. Mr. Warren shook his head slowly from side to side and then said, "Shit."

* * *

What I remember about the first time I met Miss Lyla Case was that my eyes got watery and my mouth took on an awful dryness. Miss Lyla Case was beautiful. She was tall, only an inch or so shorter than me; she had dark hair that fell in little waterfalls around her neck and shoulders and sometimes in the wind it reached around and brushed against her face. Her eyes, too, were dark and her skin was not the wool white that seemed to be favoured by women then, and by the men who watched them; instead, it was a light coffee colour and if you'll pardon me for saying so, I drank her in every opportunity I had.

The first of those opportunities came immediately after her arrival. She did what most new arrivals did and stopped in at the store. There were two reasons for this being the normal course of events. First, the store was situated immediately across from where the stagecoach stopped. And secondly, there were at that time only six commercial buildings on the street (there are a few more now), the others being the livery; the Independent Cities Hotel, which was at the far end of the street; the combined office of Mr. Warren and Dr. Philip Fenster, the town's Englishman doctor; the National Land and Grain office (the stagecoach stopped in front of it — I never knew why); and Martel's Implement and Tool Supply, a new store that has cut into J. Harper Westover's General Store profits since we also sell implements and tools. Mr. Westover claimed Martel was just a failed farmer who couldn't make a living in the fields so had taken up stealing from us. When he said that, and he said it fairly often, I didn't bother to point out that

Mr. Westover, himself, once had a farm back in Ohio that people say didn't do very well mostly because Mr. Westover insisted on planting crops that wouldn't grow in Ohio's climate.

I suppose of the six businesses that could be seen on Main Street — there was a restaurant and a barber shop in the lobby of the Independent Cities Hotel and you know about the bar, but you couldn't see any of them until you were inside the building — our store was the most inviting to a new arrival in town.

The day Miss Lyla Case stepped down from the stage, Mr. Westover, who spent most of his time playing cards over at the hotel, happened to be in the store. Nettie Whitman was also there examining ladies undergarments and so was Cooper Raine, the hotel clerk/barber who was pretending to be looking over the latest dime novels to come in but actually was sneaking peeks every chance he got at the items Nettie was holding up in front of herself.

I was thinking Cooper had better be careful; Nettie Whitman was a hard minded woman. A lot of folks in town claimed she was a person of ... loose morality ... and it's true that most of the young men in town (I regret to have to include myself in that group) got their first look at a naked lady by watching Nettie getting ready for bed in front of her bedroom window which for as long as I can remember was without curtains.

On one particular occasion, some of the town boys — I would have been one of them, but my father had me doing extra chores that night — broke the front window of Nettie's house and threw a live hog into her living room. Where they made their mistake was they stayed around to watch the fun. Nettie went for a rifle she kept in the hall and the boys thought she was going to shoot that hog. But she walked right by the pig, went straight to the window and fired a round of buckshot into the fleshiest part of Billy Mitchell as he was trying to scramble over Nettie's picket fence. To this day, Billy is the slowest person in town at sitting down and standing up, except for Archie Cuddy who has the arthritis pretty bad in his hips. You can see why I say Cooper Raine didn't want to be taking liberties with Nettie.

Of course, when Miss Lyla Case walked into the store, I had no idea who she was. I had assumed that Mr. Warren, after his conversation with Teacher, had written a letter to the second school teacher he'd hired telling her she wouldn't be needed. But, for some reason, he hadn't done that. He said afterward he'd meant to but forgot. I'm not at all sure he was telling the truth about that. I think he was maybe hoping that the arrival of Miss Lyla Case might embarrass Teacher into leaving.

She was standing in front of me, smiling. I already mentioned about my eyes watering and my mouth being dry. But then I also became conscious of the fact that if I didn't soon take a breath, I was going to pass out. So, I breathed.

"Hello, I'm Lyla Case, I'm the new teacher," she said. "I'm hoping you might be the gentleman who has the lodgings."

I stopped breathing again. But my brain didn't stop working. As a matter of fact, it was working very fast. My mouth was working too, although slower, maybe from the dryness. And not in sentences.

"Lodgings ... uh ... house ... yes'm, we were ... not expecting you ... that is, *were* yes, were expecting you, Miss ..."

"Case. Lyla Case." She held out the loveliest hand that had ever reached over the counter of J. Harper Westover's General Store.

I looked at it for a very long time. Cooper Raine coughed. I looked up and saw he was looking back at me over a piece of ladies wearing apparel Nettie Whitman was admiring. He was pointing at Miss Lyla Case's hand. I took the hand, which felt as good as it looked, and moved it slowly up and down.

"But ..." I said.

"But?" she repeated.

"But?" I repeated.

"You said but."

"I did?" I looked over at Cooper Raine who had popped up next to a pink item Nettie was unfolding. He nodded at me again.

"Yes, well, I did say 'but'. But what I meant was ... actually ... "

Miss Lyla Case looked at me the way mothers look at their children when they have yelled out in church.

"You said 'but' when you meant 'actually'?" she said.

"Yes."

"Actually, what?"

"Actually, there's a man there already."

"In the room that has been reserved for me?"

"No, not actually, but ..."

"We're back to those two words again."

"What I mean is, there is a man in the house ... already ... actually."

"Besides you."

"Besides me, yes, ma'am."

"I don't see that as a problem. The last boarding house I stayed at had several gentlemen guests. I assume that this person *is* a gentleman."

"Oh, yes, ma'am he is that, but ..."

"Excuse me, my name is Cooper Raine." Cooper stepped out from the ladies wear aisle leaving Nettie to continue her examination of feminine undergarments on her own. He walked, very noisily I thought, to the counter where Miss Lyla Case and I were talking. Normally, I'm not at all happy to be interrupted by Cooper's chatter especially since a lot of the time it makes no sense. But this was one time that the sound of Cooper's irritating voice was the most pleasant sound I could imagine.

I looked at Cooper and waited for him to say something more. The trouble was, once he got close to Miss Lyla Case, he seemed to be struck down with a lot of the same afflictions that I had. The result was silence. Miss Lyla Case looked at Cooper Raine expecting, I suppose, that he would speak again. But Cooper Raine, the most talkative person in the history of Kecking Horse, was speechless. What he was doing, instead of talking, was looking at Miss Lyla Case and blinking. Watery eyes, I thought to myself. His mouth was opening and closing every few seconds, but no sounds were coming out of there. Dry mouth, I guessed. Finally, with a bigger blink than all the other ones and after what seemed like a whole afternoon of getting his voice ready to function, he spoke.

"Miss Case," said Cooper, "I couldn't help but overhear and I want you to know that as one of the town's most ... respectable citizens, I will be of service to you in whatever way I can."

Miss Lyla Case didn't seem to have any idea what Cooper's being respectable had to do with any of this. Neither did I.

"I'm very glad to hear it, Mr. Raine," said Miss Lyla Case and turned back to me. "Now, about my accommodations."

"Yes," I said.

"Yes," said Cooper Raine.

"I'd like to go there now with your permission so that I may clean up after the journey."

"Of course you have ... may," I said.

"Of course," Cooper agreed.

Miss Lyla Case turned a wonderful smile on Cooper. "Perhaps, Mr. Raine," she said in a voice that reminded me of soft snow falling, "you would be so kind as to make arrangements to have my trunk and bags taken to my place of residence."

"Oh," said Cooper.

It was about then I realized that the problem of two teachers for one one-room school was not mine to solve. That was up to Mr. Marcus Warren. The thought made me feel a lot better and I was able to concentrate totally on the beauty of Miss Lyla Case and the discomfort of Cooper Raine.

"Yes, Cooper," I said. "You're the very one to look after Miss Lyla Case's things."

You have to remember that although Cooper Raine was always in the middle of things as they were happening, he never actually *did* anything himself. I remember my pa once saying that Cooper Raine and work were like a stud horse and a mare that wasn't in season — you could encourage all you wanted but you'd never get them together.

As Miss Lyla Case and I made our way out into the street and toward the house, I was thinking about what the evening would bring, what with Mother and the two teachers, one male and one female, both hired for the same job all sitting around the parlor after dinner. But it didn't turn out to be all that interesting an event after all. Never really had a chance to be.

That was the night someone tried to kill Virgil Watts.

Chapter Four

It happened very much the same way it had with my pa. Prince came running into town all in a lather and nobody saw at first, because it was dark, that Watts was hanging from one stirrup. They got Prince stopped in front of the hotel and it was Jake Drury and Cooper Raine who pulled Watts free.

Once Jake discovered who the injured person was, he turned and marched back into the hotel leaving Watts bleeding in the street. Cooper had the good sense to hustle off and get Doc Fenster. Then, after he and the doctor and a couple of other people who were standing around got Watts to the doctor's office, Cooper came to the house to fetch Teacher.

I went along and when we got to Doc Fenster's office and walked in, I came awful close to being sick to my stomach. I couldn't have said for sure who the man on Doc Fenster's table was if I'd been there by myself. He was blood from the top of his head right down to his waist. Even his hands were soaked red.

Doc Fenster looked up when he saw us come in. "He's alive but I'm not sure why. Or for how long." That's all he said, then he turned back and went on working over Watts' battered body.

I couldn't see any way the man — or any man for that matter — could survive what had happened to him. I'd seen my pa in almost exactly the same condition seven years before and my pa was one of the toughest men I'd ever known, not tough like in fighting, but tough in spirit and wanting to live and those things. And he died less than an hour after we pulled him free of the mare.

Cooper Raine could have been reading my thoughts. "It's just like what happened to your pa." He looked at the destruction that was Virgil Watts. "He must've been drug, God knows how far. It was that damn killer horse Archie Cuddy sold him. I hope somebody—"

"Maybe," Teacher said, "maybe not. We'll see."

For once I was inclined to agree with Cooper. I'd seen Prince in action that day in the pasture out of town and if there was ever a horse I'd pick to try to hurt a man bad, that'd be the horse. I guess if Watts had died that's what most folks would have thought. Just a strange coincidence that two such similar accidents could happen like that is what we would've said.

Except that Watts didn't die. In fact, the next day he was sitting up in Doc Fenster's office talking through lips that looked like pink oatmeal trying to tell Teacher what had happened. He had to repeat most everything three or four times, but I won't write all of that here. I'll just give you the main part of the conversation as best I recollect it.

"I got jumped," Watts said. "Three men."

"Did you get a look at them?"

Watts shook his head. "It was dark, and they knocked me pert near senseless early on with a board or something. After that, things was mighty fuzzy. But I kind of come to from time to time and one of those times was when they was hangin' me up in my saddle. They wedged my foot in the stirrup so's there'd be no way I could get free. Then they put the run on Prince, and I reckon I must've passed out not long after the draggin' started."

"Where'd it happen?" Teacher asked.

"Line camp on the north edge of the 40 is where they jumped me. I was checkin' a bunch of steers that was stickin' around Medicine Creek."

I looked up then. Of course, the 40 wasn't far from where we used to ranch, but I hadn't thought until right then, how it was in that same country my pa's accident had happened. You'll remember, I told you earlier I've always had a doubt or two in my mind about his death being an accident. And now this. Of course, what was confusing about the whole thing was the fact that naturally I figured Waincastle and Cook had something to do with what happened to Watts. And neither of them were in the territory when Pa was killed. They'd only been working at the Bar U for a couple of years. So maybe I was wrong about the two draggings being related. Still, it made you think. Or it could've been that some people didn't take to a black man living and working in the area. That was a possibility too.

Teacher was all for riding up to that line camp right then to see if he could find anything, but Watts told him he was sure the men who'd jumped him would have moved on and covered their tracks. Teacher agreed but I noticed he didn't want to.

* * *

I've just been reading this over and realize I've hardly mentioned the school. You see, there wasn't one. At least not right then. The plan was that we'd use the old Ramsay farm bunkhouse, for the first while, until the new schoolhouse could be built. We'd had a big work bee out at the Ramsay place — Ramsay and his family packed up and moved back to Kansas the year before. I'd have to say we had the bunkhouse looking real scholarly by the end of the day and a lot of us figured it would do for a year or two anyway.

But that wasn't what Mr. Warren had in mind. No, Sir. No bunkhouse would do as a school in his jurisdiction. And when Mr. Marcus Warren set his mind on something, he generally got what he wanted (except in the matter of hiring teachers, of course). So, he reluctantly agreed to allow school to take place for a month in the Ramsay bunkhouse on the understanding that the new Kecking Horse School would be open to students in no more than four weeks.

The site of the new school was a couple of miles further west on the dirt road that led to the 40 Ranch. There was a pretty little spot just this side of the 40 that Mr. Warren decided was the ideal location. The land didn't actually belong to anybody except the government, and there was a little creek that ran through it with saskatoon, chokecherry, and huckleberry bushes all through there. The first time Teacher saw the spot, he said, "Maybe Mr. Warren figures if I can't teach the kids anything, at least they won't starve to death."

The first work bee for the new school took place the day before the first lessons were to be taught at the Ramsay bunkhouse. As far as I knew, nothing had been done to resolve the oversupply of teachers situation so I was as surprised as anybody when during the supper break, Mr. Warren stood up, brushed chicken crumbs off his shirt and cleared his throat loudly enough for everyone to get the idea that he wanted to say something.

"Ladies and Gentlemen ... and soon-to-be students (some polite laughter here), I am pleased to inform you that I have been able to bring a successful resolution to the misunderstanding that has existed up to now concerning who will be charged with the responsibility of illuminating the bright young minds of our children (a look here at some of the kids who were sitting here and there, quite a few of them making faces of a disrespectful sort). Beginning tomorrow, our students will have the benefit of not one, but two, fine teachers (some applause, not all that enthusiastic, and a lot of looks exchanged between folks). Miss Case will teach in the morning and she will instruct in numbers, Latin and music. Our ... other teacher will be with the students in the afternoon and will see to letters and history. And, of course, in only one month we will be moving into our brand new school" (a look over his shoulder to the framework, most of which was in place after just one afternoon's work).

Mr. Warren went on for some time about the virtues of community spirit and working together — most of us figured it was so he wouldn't have to say much more about the unheard of idea of two teachers for maybe fifteen students — and finally sat down to resume his attack on Nettie Whitman's basket of chicken. There was no applause at the end of the speech, no doubt because most of us were trying to figure out how the citizens of Kecking Horse were going to be able to afford to pay two teachers.

I found out later that the negotiations had been conducted between Teacher, Miss Lyla Case and Mother, and that Mr. Warren hadn't even been involved until everything was pretty much resolved. What was decided was that Teacher and Miss Lyla Case would split one salary, but that Mother would help out by offering free board to both of them for the first three months. To be honest, I wasn't particularly pleased by Mother's generosity, especially as I was the one who was supposed to be receiving the board money. Everyone else seemed reasonably pleased with the arrangements, especially Mr. Marcus Warren, who didn't have to try to get out of the situation he'd worked himself into.

Mr. Warren was to be disappointed on one point, however. The schedule for moving into the new school received a setback the very night of that first work bee. The frame of the new school and a lot of the wood that had been cut and stacked for future work bees was destroyed by fire, every stick burned to ashes. Most of us figured the fire was set deliberately, though no one could think why anyone would want to keep the new school from being built.

After that, Teacher declined the free board from Mother and set up a little camp at the site of the new school. He stayed there whenever he wasn't teaching. To tell the truth, I breathed a little easier with him gone from our house, just because of the delicate arrangement that existed with Miss Lyla Case living there at the same time. Cooper Raine said it was just selfishness, that I wanted her all to myself, but that, of course, was ridiculous. I never thought for even a moment that Miss Lyla Case would give me so much as a second look. But by now you've become well enough acquainted with Cooper to know that if something really dumb needs saying, he's the man for the job.

Virgil Watts couldn't go back to work right away so he moved into Teacher's old room for a few days while he healed up. I learned a lot about him during that time, even though at first, he was reluctant to talk about himself. When he finally did, what he told was an amazing story. He related all about his parents being slaves in South Carolina and how after the Civil War he'd traveled around and fought in boxing matches against other black men for the entertainment of rich white folks. Then he'd headed out to Texas, which was where he first began developing his skill as a cowhand. The next few things he told me surprised me even more than the stuff he'd already talked about. Like the fact that he'd been in Montana before, after he'd helped trail a herd from Texas up to the Bitterroot Valley Country. From there he'd gone up to Canada. And if you can believe it — fifteen years ago or so he worked on the Bar U — wouldn't that have given Cook and Waincastle a bad case of saddle sores if they'd known about it.

But that wasn't the part that amazed me most. That came when he told me he was married with two children. I don't know why that surprised me. I guess it's just that he rode into town like most of the bachelor cowboys do — looking for a job and not mentioning anything about a family. Turns out his wife and children were up in Canada somewhere. He'd left them there for the previous couple of years when everything had been so dry, and he'd gone south to find work. He had been punching cows down around Dodge City and that's where he met up with Teacher. Teacher was heading north for the teaching job and Watts was wanting to rejoin his family, so they decided to travel together.

Naturally I asked him, "How come you didn't keep going right on up north to Canada? Why'd you stop off here?"

"I figured I'd stick around just till my friend gets a few things straightened up." That's what he said which, of course, I puzzled over when I first heard it.

"What things?" I asked him, but he just shrugged and changed the subject. What he changed it to caught me pretty much off guard. In fact, I was to find out later he hadn't changed the subject at all.

"You know anything about a man named Matt Slater?" he asked.

You know, I'd almost forgotten completely about that. I shouldn't have since it was a pretty famous dying at the time, which was about a year and a half or so before.

"Not much," I said. "They found him half underwater in the creek not far from where the new school is being built. He'd been shot once in the back of the head. That's about it."

"You know 'im at all?"

"Not really," I shook my head. "Met him a couple of times. He came into the store now and again. Nice enough fella. Quiet."

"Any idea why somebody would want to kill him?" Watts asked me.

"Nope, he was most likely robbed," I said. "Of course, Cooper Raine has a bunch of theories, but I imagine ..."

"What sort?"

"What?"

"Them theories of Raine's. What sort were they?"

"I'm not sure of them all," I said. "Everything from how Slater discovered gold and got ambushed for it to somebody just killing him for the sheer hell-pleasure of it. Sort of along the lines of what happened to... "

"Me," Watts finished the thought. Then he nodded slowly like he was thinking something particular.

"And my pa, though it happened a long time ago," I added. "Why do you ask anyway?"

"No special reason. Just heard the name and got to wondering about it."

Naturally, I thought he figured there might be something to connect what had happened to him with the killing of Matt Slater. There were a few similarities, all right. They happened in the same part of the country. And there was no doubt that whoever had jumped Watts had wanted him to be dead. I lay awake for a long time that night and thought about the violence our town had known over the years. Which, of course, got me thinking about my pa and my throat kind of tightened up like it always does when I think about him.

I have trouble going to sleep when I'm feeling bad so to make myself cheer up, I let my thoughts drift off in the direction of Miss Lyla Case. Then I went to sleep.

Chapter Five

J. Emerson Keymore didn't come to town very often. People said he was something of a hermit although I personally never held with that suggestion. It didn't make sense if you thought about it since his ranch, the J Reverse K, was the second biggest in the territory next to the Bar U, and since the Bar U wasn't exactly in this territory, I guess that made the J Reverse K the biggest. I figured it would be just about impossible to live like a hermit with twenty or thirty people working for you. Naturally, Cooper Raine thought he had the answer to why the man who everybody said was the richest for five hundred miles in any direction didn't often come to town.

"He's harbouring some deep secret," Cooper told me once while I was sorting leather goods in the back of the store. "Something he doesn't want anyone to know."

"Like what?" I didn't bother to look up from the headstalls and chaps.

"Who knows? Hidden money, a terrible past, guilty conscience, hell, maybe he killed somebody and has 'im buried out there ..."

There was more. There always is with Cooper but I won't bother you with it all. That's the gist of it anyhow. Anyway, a couple of days after school classes started in the Ramsay bunkhouse, J. Emerson Keymore rode into town. He had five men with him. Cook and Waincastle were two of them. Naturally, I went to thinking about that, since Cook and Waincastle were Bar U hands. The other men with Mr. Keymore, I'd never seen before.

One thing about having Cooper Raine around is that anything that is even remotely interesting, and a lot of stuff that isn't, gets circulated around to everybody in a very short time. It's like having a human newspaper, one of those gossipy ones that are so popular nowadays. Mr. Keymore wasn't in town for twenty minutes when Cooper Raine burst into the store all out of breath.

"Keymore's hired Cook and Waincastle away from the Bar U and those other three from some outfit east of here. Their names are Carruthers, Mayes and ... I can't think of the other one's name but ..." (at this point Cooper looked around and put his hand up alongside his mouth). "They're askin' about Teacher and Watts."

"Asking as in Mr. Keymore wants to hire them too?" I tried not to look too interested because I hate giving Cooper the satisfaction.

"Nope." He looked around a second time. "Askin' as in me an' the boys want to have a talk with 'em."

"Teacher's at school," I said. "He's teaching right now. Then he'll be out at the new school site. You'd think they'd know that. And Watts has gone back cowboyin' out at the—"

Cooper waved his hand impatiently. He was no different than most people who love to hear themselves. He didn't enjoy listening to anyone else near as much.

"I know all that," he said. "I told them all that."

"What'd they say?"

"They went off to look for Mr. Warren. But I heard Keymore say something about gettin' rid of that damn school. That's exactly what he said...'damn school'."

With that the two-legged Gazette-Times-Chronicle was out the door and headed for his next audience.

Of course, what none of us knew was that Teacher had been working early mornings and evenings on the new school and just about had the framing back to where it was before the fire. It was at least another couple of hours before Cooper came by with that piece of news. But what was more interesting was that J. Emerson Keymore seemed to be more upset than anybody that we had two school teachers, and that one of them was a man.

None of this made any sense to me. Why would J. Emerson Keymore ride all the way into town to complain about the running of the school when he didn't even have any kids? And why would he want to take up the matter with Teacher? It wasn't Teacher's fault that Mr. Warren had hired two teachers. Why had Mr.

Keymore asked for Teacher *and* Watts? And why had he brought along all the tough looking cowboys? I posed these questions to Cooper, but he was already thinking about who he would tell next and left without answering.

When I got the store closed that night, I decided to take a ride out to the new school site to talk to Teacher. I figured he better at least know what's going on and Cooper's information service didn't extend that far out of town. Of course, riding out there after work meant I'd have to pass up a fried chicken dinner with Miss Lyla Case (and Mother), which was a pretty big sacrifice.

Teacher was sitting by the fire drinking a cup of coffee and reading a book when I rode up. As we exchanged greetings, I noticed he had a rifle leaning against a nearby stump and the .44 was sitting on a rock right in front of him.

"The framing looks real fine." I waved in the direction of the work he'd been doing.

"Thanks," he said. "You had dinner?"

"Yep, two helpings," I told him, "but you go ahead with yours." I'm not sure why people lie about things like that. Truth is I was starving. The ride and thinking about Miss Lyla Case and all that fried chicken had made me feel mighty gaunt as I sat down alongside Teacher.

He was enjoying biscuits he'd made just a few minutes before. I noticed he liked them slathered in honey, same way I do. For the next fifteen minutes we didn't talk much. Teacher ate quite a few biscuits and some bacon he'd fried up. We both drank coffee. I felt that Teacher was enjoying the evening more than I was.

Finally, he looked over at me. "That wasn't your stomach growling, was it?"

"Naw," I said. "Couldn't've been."

"Well," he said, "I just can't finish those last few biscuits. Hate to throw 'em to the birds, but I guess if you're too full from dinner ..."

"Well, I hate to see good biscuits go for birdfeed." I wanted him to think I was only accepting the biscuits as a favour to him. But, I might've ate 'em a little too fast to be convincing. The biscuits gave me a little more strength to talk and I told Teacher about the visit of Mr. Keymore and what he'd said about the school and Teacher and Watts.

He nodded a couple of times while I was talking but mostly he drank his coffee and watched the night dark settle over the camp.

When I'd finished, he said, "You ever hear tell of a man called Matt Slater?"

It was the second time I'd been asked that question in the last few days, first Watts and now Teacher. I figured there had to be something important about the man who'd got himself shot a few days after he arrived here.

I repeated what I'd told Watts, that Matt Slater had been killed and left not far from where we were sitting right at that moment.

Teacher pointed behind us with his coffee cup. "Right through there, as a matter of fact."

"Really?" I shivered and took a long drink of the coffee. I hadn't known it was *that* close. I wondered why he asked me if he already seemed to know more about the killing of Slater than I did.

For a long time, Teacher didn't say anything. He picked up the .44 and looked at it like he was seeing it for the first time; at least that's what it seemed like to me.

I watched him for a while but finally I had to ask the question that was on my mind.

"What was Matt Slater to you and Watts?"

Teacher looked at me but didn't answer.

"I mean ..., well, it's just that both of you have asked me about him and I figured ... well, I don't know what I figured but I was kind of wondering."

Teacher nodded his head real slow. "He was a U.S. Marshall. I knew him is all."

"Was he investigating a case up here or something? Looking for somebody, was he?"

The man I was drinking coffee with around that campfire was a very different person from the one who'd laughed so hard at Virgil Watts' attempts to tame a wild horse. He stared into his coffee cup as he said, "I wouldn't know about that. But if I should come across the man that shot Matt Slater in the back of the head, I'll have to kill that man."

An idea started to work its way round the corners of my mind. "You really a teacher?"

He looked at me and the grin I'd been used to seeing suddenly returned. The dancing light of the flames from the campfire made it look like the grin was moving around on his face.

"Well, let's just say that if Mr. Warren had really checked out those references I sent, I don't think I would've got this job."

I stood up. "I guess I better be making my way back to town. It'll be pretty late by the time I get back."

Teacher threw the last of his coffee into the fire and stood up. "I appreciate your riding out here to tell me about Keymore."

"He's got Cook and Waincastle and some other tough looking people riding for him." I stepped up into the saddle. "You sure staying out here by yourself is such a good idea?"

Teacher handed me the reins of my horse and smiled. "Drop out to the Ramsay bunkhouse some afternoon and see how I get along with all this teaching business. You might find it interesting."

I nodded and said I would. I figured I ought to say something more about the work he was doing on the new schoolhouse but I couldn't see it in the dark. So, I nodded again and turned my horse towards town.

I had a lot to think about on the way back. Things like how Teacher might not be a teacher at all and about the connection between him being here and the murder of Matt Slater. Then there was how Mr. Keymore wanted him gone and maybe that's why the school got burned down. I wasn't sure if I had it all right or even if I had *any* of it right, but the ride went quicker with all the thinking. One other thought that kept popping into my head had to do with fried chicken. Good as Teacher's biscuits were and much as I appreciated him sharing and all, I wondered whether there'd be any chicken left when I got back home.

* * *

I took Teacher up on his offer a couple of days later. Mr. Westover had given me an afternoon off for working some extra hours, which I did every year about that time when a lot of our fall supplies came in. I ate a sandwich, drank a glass of buttermilk, and headed for the Ramsay schoolhouse.

The day was warm, almost hot. It was the kind of fall day that made me hate having to go to school when I was a kid and I was curious to see how Teacher's students would behave. When I got there, I was surprised to see that all of the students and Teacher himself were outside. The lunch break was long over, and it seemed strange they weren't inside, hunched over their slates. But there they were in the schoolyard gathered up in a group. The only voice I could hear was Teacher's. As I got closer, I could see that the students were actually gathered around a horse, a short stout grey. Teacher was bent over, holding up one of the horse's feet and he was nailing a shoe on. He saw me and waved, then made a few more taps on the shoe and set the horse's foot down.

"You can put him away, Jeremy, he'll get you home just fine now," he said.

70

A student I recognized as Jeremy Clark led the grey off toward a hitchin' post that stood not far from the front door of the school. There were several horses tied up there.

"Afternoon. You picked a good day to come," Teacher smiled at me as I got down out of the saddle. "Michael will tie up your horse for you."

I handed the reins to a tall boy with bright red hair. Teacher introduced me to the students — I knew most of them from the store — then he answered the question I hadn't had a chance to ask yet.

"It's outdoors day," he explained. "Once a week we spend the afternoon outside doing a few things that I figure might be every bit as useful as book learning. Jeremy's mare threw a shoe this morning, so that was the first piece of business. Now we're going down to the creek to learn a few tricks of survival if we're ever lost. And later it's a baseball game — you'll play, won't you?"

I'd never played baseball. In fact, I'd only seen it once when my pa played for the town team against a bunch of traveling players. I didn't relish the idea of looking like a fool in front of all these kids.

"Well ... uh ..."

"Sure you will," Teacher patted me on the shoulder. "Come on, you can help me show them how to build a shelter. Let's go."

We started off hiking at a very fast pace with Teacher talking to the students the whole

71

time. He amazed me with his knowledge of nature. He pointed out trees, flowers and birds that I'd seen all my life but didn't know the names of. Teacher not only knew their names but was aware of all kinds of interesting facts about most of them as well.

From time to time one of the kids would ask a question, like, "What's best for poison ivy?" or "Where do the eagles go in the winter?" and Teacher would answer. Good answers, too, not stupid stuff like Cooper Raine gives for answers to questions even when he isn't the one being asked.

We spent an hour down at the river, building a shelter out of deadfall and spruce branches and Teacher had all of us, even me, eat some roots he dug up. The roots weren't all that tasty, but I guess if I was lost and out of food, it was a piece of knowledge that could come in handy. He even took his knife and cut himself on the arm and showed us how if you mixed mud and spit with the pulp of one of the roots we'd been eating, you could make the bleeding stop. On the way back to the school yard, Teacher and I were walking a little ways from the students.

"How do you think Mr. Warren would take to 'outdoors day' and building shelters and eating roots and what not?"

"He'd hate it."

"Kind of what I was thinking," I nodded. "Don't you worry about him coming out here one day when you're outside doing something and—?"

"Nope."

"You don't? Why not?"

"See that dark-haired girl over there?" Teacher pointed.

"Round-faced gal? Kind of pouty looking?"

"Yeah."

"I don't think I've seen her before, or if I have...

"Her name's Betts. She's Warren's daughter."

I whistled. "Then you really are taking a chance. She's sure to tell her father sooner or later."

"I don't think so."

"Why not?"

"Well, the first time we had one of these outdoors days, I did a little thing with a magnifying glass and spontaneous combustion. Started a little grass fire and we got some good practice putting it out. Turns out none of these kids had ever seen anything like that before. So, I just happened to let slip that at my last school, a student got way out of line in his behavior, and I got so mad I made him burst into flames." Teacher grinned real big at me. "Haven't had much in the way of discipline problems since. Everybody was quite impressed by my little demonstration, Betts Warren most of all."

I thought about what he'd said for quite a while before I said anything.

"Did you really?"

"What?"

"Set a kid on fire ... at your last school?"

Teacher's grin faded and he looked at me for a long time. Then he fished in his pocket and pulled out a piece of glass.

He held it out to me. "You ever see one of these before?"

"Well, I've seen glass before."

"This is a magnifying glass" Teacher held it closer. "You know what that means?"

"Of course. It magnifies things," I didn't want him thinking I was some kind of dull witted country boy.

"That's right," Teacher smiled, "but have you ever seen what else it can do?"

"I ... guess not."

"I thought as much," Teacher put the glass back in his pocket, then didn't say anything more for quite a while.

We were almost back to the school and I needed to know. "Well?"

"Well, what?"

"Your last school. That kid you set on fire. What happened to him?"

Teacher patted his pocket where the glass was. "Let's just say it would be best if you didn't ever make me real mad."

I looked at him, but I couldn't tell if he was smiling or not. It wasn't until we were in the middle of the baseball game that I remembered our conversation at the campfire when he'd hinted that maybe there hadn't been any previous school, but all that did was to confuse me even more in my thinking about Teacher.

The baseball game wasn't the best part of my day. I figured Teacher must have had those kids playing ball prior to that afternoon because every single one of them, including Betts Warren, was better at it than me.

We chose up sides and my team suffered for having me as a member. I dropped the ball every time it came my way; I never did figure out how to throw the thing and have it go where I was aiming. I wasn't much better at batting. In fact, the only time I succeeded in getting the bat to strike the ball, it didn't go far, and Betts Warren picked it up and tossed it to the tall redheaded kid so I was 'out'. That's the term they use in baseball to describe what happened to me every time I got up to bat.

It was fun, I suppose, even if I wasn't much good at it. I took comfort from the fact that Cooper Raine hadn't been there to see the game, so at least my lack of baseball playing skills wouldn't be the subject of conversation in every building in town by that evening.

It was interesting to see the way Teacher got on with the students. He laughed with them, talked with them, listened to them and answered their questions. What stood out most of all was how much he seemed to like them. And they liked him back. Spontaneous combustion or not. I wondered if things went as well when he was teaching the more traditional subjects in the classroom. One other thing I wondered was what Mr. Warren thought about the fact that Teacher still had the .44 strapped on his hip. It had even been there during the baseball game.

"You'll stay for supper," he said once the students had all headed for home on foot or horseback.

"Thanks, but I better not." I shook my head. "It's getting dark earlier now and I think I should be getting along. I promised Mother I'd husk some corn for supper." That gave me an idea. "Why don't you come back to town with me and join us for supper. I know Mother won't mind."

Teacher shook his head. "I appreciate the offer but I kind of like to be around that new schoolhouse building at night in case anybody gets any ideas."

"Sure, I understand." We walked over to my horse. "Looks to me like you're a born teacher," I told him as I mounted up.

Teacher laughed real hard at that although I couldn't see the humour in what I'd said.

"So long." he slapped my horse lightly on the hip.

I waved and headed off toward town as the sun was dipping behind the hills to the west. I figure I was about halfway back to town when they ambushed me.

The light was pretty well gone which is why I never knew how many of them there were; I think maybe four, three for sure. They didn't say anything, just rode up alongside and knocked me off my horse. It happened so fast I didn't have time to do much or say much except "What do you think you're doing?" Then they got off their horses and started beating and kicking me. I tried to fight back but I'm not much of a fighter and I don't think any of the punches I threw hit anybody. When it was over, my hands were about the only part of me that didn't hurt.

I figure what must've saved me was a couple of wild horses. That, and how I happened to be wearing boots that were a couple of sizes too big. Whoever jumped me, after they beat me up for a while, hung me up in my stirrup just like they had done with Watts. I know that because my boot was still in that stirrup when Teacher found me. And right next to my horse was a couple of wild mustangs that must have strayed off from the main herd that ranges mostly north of here. They were mares, curious mares at that; Teacher figured Powder probably stopped to visit. That's when my foot slipped out of my boot and I landed on the ground next to a clump of sage.

Teacher never told me exactly why he happened along, said something about having second thoughts about the corn on the cob, but I was never sure whether he really meant that or if he'd actually been going someplace and just stumbled across me. I was nowhere near as bad off as Watts. Maybe they meant to kill him and just scare me or maybe my dragging getting cut short was what saved me. Anyway, I was mostly okay except for a lot of scrapes and bruises and the bad part, a broken nose. I say the bad part because ever since that night I've always felt I had the look of a pale, skinny pelican. And pelicans aren't likely to be successful in attracting women the likes of Miss Lyla Case.

The other thing that came out of my being jumped was that Teacher got real mad, even madder than before and this time there was no talking him out of doing something about it. I guess I was partly responsible for that too. I happened to notice — it's about the only thing I did recollect out of that night — silver cheek pieces on the bridle of the horse of one of my attackers.

I don't know how it came about that a couple of round pieces of silver, probably not much bigger than a silver dollar, caught my attention in the dark and confusion, but I was absolutely positive about those cheek pieces. I mentioned them to Teacher after he got me back to town and after I got myself sorted out enough to talk. (My voice was different too with that broken nose and all the cotton swabs Doc Fenster stuffed up my nostrils — I sounded like I had a bad cold.) Anyway, after I told Teacher about that one detail that was fixed in my memory, it wasn't long before he rode out.

He waited though until he was satisfied that I was all right. (He wouldn't take my word for it — he had to hear it direct from Doc Fenster.) Then he was gone, and we didn't hear from him for a couple of days. I guess it's a good thing the next day was Saturday or he would have been missed at school. As it was, nobody saw him until Sunday night when he rode through town on his way back to the camp.

What I just wrote is not quite true. In fact, I found out later, from Teacher himself and others that quite a few people saw him. For example, J. Emerson Keymore saw Teacher. Waincastle saw him. Cook saw him, too. And one of Mr. Keymore's new hands, a man named Link Mayes, saw a whole lot of Teacher. It turned out Link Mayes had a real nice set of silver cheek pieces on the bridle of his horse and matching silver jingle bobs on his spurs. Teacher didn't appear to care much about the spurs, but he took a particular interest in the cheek pieces. When he asked Mayes about what he'd been doing and where he'd been about the time I got jumped, Link took it in his head to sass Teacher something awful and call him a couple of names that don't generally come up in conversation around my mother's dinner table. That wasn't too smart on Mayes' part, as it turned out.

It was about that time, I'm told, that Teacher took a fence post from a pile that was sittin' there and drove the pointy end into Mayes' stomach, which I'm inclined to think must have hurt pretty bad. But then Teacher turned the post and used it kind of like the baseball bat we had used in our game and hit Mayes three or four times around the head and the last hit he made sure broke Mayes' nose. I saw Mayes sometime afterward and he didn't resemble a pelican anywhere near as much as me, but it was easy enough to tell his nose had been broken. Now the story is that there were at least five or six men, all friends of Mayes or men he worked with, watching this take place (only two or three when Teacher told it) but not one of them cared to interfere at all or even go for his gun.

After that, the kind of stuff that had happened to Watts and me didn't take place for a good while. I don't know if everybody feared Teacher or what, but I never saw him challenged, not by men in groups of two or three and not even by Mr. J. Emerson Keymore himself, who was pretty much fearless even though he was probably well into his sixties at the time.

And so, things were kind of peaceful for a time.

Chapter Six

There was some good and some bad that came out of what happened to me. Miss Lyla Case took it upon herself to become my personal nurse whenever she wasn't at school. This I found to be very good and it more than made up for the pain (truth is, there wasn't much) of my injuries. What was a whole lot worse was the regular afternoon visit of Cooper Raine who made it his business to drop by daily to bring the news.

Most of the time there wasn't any of that either, but that didn't stop Cooper from coming around about three o'clock every single afternoon. He always led off the conversation with "Where's Miss Lyla today?" I'd noticed that Miss Lyla Case, after a few visits from Cooper, managed to be busy in some remote part of the house whenever he came by.

The fact that my injuries looked a lot worse than they hurt allowed me to remain bedridden for longer than I needed to be — I admit it now and I suppose I'm a little ashamed — and to receive the benefit of Miss Lyla Case's gentle care. I wouldn't go so far as to say I pretended to be hurt when I wasn't, just to keep Miss Lyla close by longer than necessary, but I suppose it's true that I didn't exactly rush my recovery.

Teacher dropped by a couple of times a week as well. We talked about a lot of different things and it was during that time — then and later when we were holed up in the schoolhouse, that I came to know him a lot better. Though I'll admit right now that there was always a lot more about Teacher that I didn't know than what I did.

He seemed to enjoy teasing me. For example, he figured out real quick that I wasn't hurt half as bad as Watts had been, but I was laid up twice as long. I explained that I was concerned about reinjuring myself if I went back to work too soon.

Teacher laughed for quite a while about that. "How much danger is a person's nose in when he's wrapping linens?" he asked me.

One night we talked for a very long time about women.

"You ever been in love?" I asked.

"Have you?" he said.

"Well ... yeah, I think so ... once," I said.

"It happens," he said.

I think he had some idea I was talking about Miss Lyla Case, which of course, was a reasonable assumption. But the fact is it wasn't her. I'm a bit nervous putting this down for folks to read especially since those folks could include Mother or even Miss Lyla Case herself. But I told it to Teacher, so I suppose I best put it down here.

"I've been with a woman," I said. "You know what I mean by 'been with'?" He nodded. "She was ... a ... sporting woman." I always hated the word whore. "Her name was Julie and she was beautiful and ... soft, not at all like I thought one of those ladies would be."

Teacher nodded but he didn't say anything.

"It happened two times," I said. "The first time Cooper Raine and some other fellas got together and paid Julie some money. Of course, I didn't know anything about it or even that she was a ...

"She came by the store and asked me if I'd stroll with her a while. Problem is there aren't a whole bunch of places you can stroll to in a place the size of Kecking Horse so after an hour or so of walking and talking our way up and down Main Street, we found ourselves at Julie's door and she asked me if I'd care to drink a cup of coffee with her. Well, I cared to quite a lot but, of course, those fellas hadn't paid Julie four dollars just to stroll and drink coffee."

Teacher smiled then but it wasn't a smile that was poking fun at me, so I felt I could go on telling him.

"I'm not sure I can recall exactly how it all happened. But one thing led to another and the next thing I do remember for sure is standing in front of Julie in my long underwear — it was February at the time — and I was awful embarrassed partly because, even in my underwear, I was considerably overdressed compared to what Julie was wearing as we stood there facing each other." I stopped talking and wiped the back of my neck which had become uncomfortably warm all of a sudden.

"I don't think I care to say any more about that evening," I said.

"No need to say anything you don't feel like," Teacher said.

I'd said I didn't want to talk about it, but the truth is that's exactly what I wanted to do.

"Maybe ... I guess it sort of feels good to talk about it," I said. "I never have before. I told you I was with Julie twice. The second time didn't have anything to do with those other guys paying for me. I went to her room on my own and tapped on her door — it was three or four days after that first time — and when she came to the door, I handed her the money and said hello. I wasn't sure what else I should say.

"She looked at me kind of surprised and then she said I could come in since she was alone. I hadn't considered that she might not be alone. I'd never thought about the fact that a man could go to see a sporting lady and find she was engaged in sporting with somebody else. I guess I figured a woman sported with one man for a time and then went to another. Mind you, I was only nineteen at the time. I'm a lot more knowledgeable now."

Teacher nodded when I said that.

"Anyway, I stayed for a very long time — a lot longer than the first time — and we talked, she cooked a meal and we ate together, and she told me about her life and her dreams. She told me how her grandmother and grandfather came north from Texas back in the thirties. They no sooner got up into this country than word came that war had broken out between the Texans and the Mexicans. So, Julie's grandfather, she never told me his name, I don't think, got back on his horse and left his wife and two young ones holding down a homestead in Judith Basin and rode all the way back to Texas. He got himself killed at the Alamo with Crockett and Travis and the others.

"Julie's grandmother, her name was Ruth, married again and very late in life had a daughter she called Alice. That was Julie's mother. When Alice was fourteen years old, her pa had died and her mother; that was Ruth, you understand, was ill when into the yard rides a mountain man called Clymer and he suggests to Ruth that he ought to take her daughter and ride off with her. Ruth wasn't about to allow that and insisted that Clymer marry Alice before he took her off to the mountains. The mountain man must've wanted the girl bad enough to agree. So, they got married, rode up into the mountains and eventually had five kids. Julie was the last one, but she was raised by a family of ranchers because Alice up and shot the mountain man one day and went to jail for it — though it sounded to me like Clymer was a man that needed shooting."

I'd been talking for some time — maybe the longest I'd ever talked all at once — and I needed to stop and take a breath or two. I was hoping Teacher wouldn't think I was getting like Cooper Raine. But he was watching me and smoking and looking like he wanted to hear the end of my story, so I went on.

"Julie told me she never wanted to be a ... bad woman, but she'd taken up with a man who promised her a nice life in California. This man was a gambler and he left her in Eureka, Oregon and Julie had no way of staying alive but to sport for a living. And there was bad luck too. Julie decided to go after that gambler and make him keep his word. But somehow, she got on the wrong stage out of Eureka — it was night and dark and all — and found herself first in Missoula and eventually Kecking Horse.

"But it was her dream that I found mighty interesting. She sang for me that night as we lay together and she was a beautiful singer. What she wanted more than anything was to get to New York and take proper training and sing on the stages, the real ones, not the saloons, of New York City. She would have been good at it too. I know she would've. But she never got the chance. "

I had to stand up and walk around a little. This was the part of the story that was hardest to tell, but it was the part I most wanted to talk about, I guess because I'd never had a chance to talk about it before. Not to anybody. I stood by the window, not looking at Teacher at all.

"By the time I left her that night I was in love with Julie. It was almost morning and I'm afraid I had to tell my mother a lie about where

I'd been. I don't know if she believed me or not. Anyway, I made plans to work hard in the store for a few years, save my money and take Julie off to New York so she could get the training and have that career in singing that she wanted.

"But, like I said, we never got the chance. A few nights after I'd been with her that second time, one of her customers didn't feel like paying and when they argued about it, he laid Julie's head open with a gun butt. She didn't live through the night.

"Sheriff Deeves rode over from Choteau, caught the man, and he was hung a month to the day after he killed Julie."

There was more I wanted to say. I wanted to tell Teacher that I wished I was the one who'd killed the man who ended Julie's dreams. But I didn't.

I know I wrote earlier some stuff about how I felt about Miss Lyla Case that first time I saw her, but, of course, that wasn't love. I don't even know if it's possible to love somebody right off like that. I did come to love Miss Lyla Case, it's true, but at the time Teacher asked me if I'd ever been in love, the only woman I'd ever loved was Julie.

"What about your dreams?" Teacher asked.

"What?"

"You told me about Julie's dreams. I'm asking about yours. What about them?"

I turned back and looked at him then. "I expect I don't have any. Not anymore."

Teacher looked like he was thinking about that. "You swim much?" he asked.

"Swim. Well, yeah, I guess some. I'm not real good at it. Kind of like baseball." I smiled.

"Did you ever notice that when you swim you don't think much about ten strokes later or even five strokes later. You only think about the stroke you're on right at this second. I think a lot of people live their days like that."

I thought it was a strange thing for him to say. I guessed he was wanting to make a particular point. But if he was, I wasn't sure I got it. "Julie didn't," I said. "She had dreams for the days she hadn't got to yet."

Teacher nodded.

"How about you?" I asked.

"What's that?"

"You didn't answer me before when I asked you if you've ever been in love. So, have you?"

It was kind of funny the way he answered that question. He shook his head at first, but then he said, "Yes, I suppose I must have been once. There was a girl, all right and I believe I did love her."

He didn't say anything more right off, but, of course, my curiosity had definitely been stirred up by what he had said.

"So, what happened? She die, or something?" I guess I was thinking about Julie. It was stupid but I figured the only two possibilities if two people were in love was either they got married or one of 'em died. I guess I hadn't thought it out all that carefully.

"She had a child," Teacher said.

"Oh," I said. Obviously in my way of thinking at that time, children went along with the first possibility, but it was obvious Teacher wasn't married since he'd answered an ad for a single school teacher.

"She wanted to get married, waited around as long as she could for me to make up my mind, but I never did. Couldn't somehow. As badly as I wanted to be with her, I couldn't seem to do the one thing I had to do to make it possible for her and me to be together."

"What was that?" I said. He'd made it sound so complicated I was getting confused. About the only things that had to happen for two people to get married was one had to ask and the other had to say yes.

"I was a United States Marshall at the time," Teacher looked at me. "I didn't want to bring her into that kind of life, and I couldn't see myself quitting my job. It was..." His voice sort of trailed off then and he didn't say anything more.

I said, "Oh," again but I couldn't think of a whole lot more to add.

Teacher filled his coffee mug from the tin coffee pot Miss Lyla Case brought me earlier. He poured some for me and leaned back in his chair.

"Seems to me I've spent a good portion of my life letting down people who were depending on me and then trying to right what

I'd done and promising myself I'd never let anything like that happen again."

Teacher often said things you didn't expect him to say, but that was a strange thing for anyone to say, especially him. I couldn't imagine him letting someone down who was counting on him except, of course, for the girl he didn't marry. And even there I could see reason behind what he did. A man puts a lot of stock in his job, especially something like a Marshall, so I could sort of see ... but then I couldn't either if I looked at it from the girl's point of view.

I noticed that dark had fallen outside, and the last part of our talk was conducted in the grey brown that comes just before the total black of night. Teacher stood up then, thanked me for the coffee and walked out without another word. I didn't go to bed until after midnight that night. Didn't feel like sleeping right away. All the same, I got up the next morning and went to work at Westover's store.

Chapter Seven

Cooper Raine took up the first couple of hours of my return to work trying to be funny. Except, what passes for humour in Cooper's mind mostly just irritates everybody else. That day was no different. He apparently felt there would be much to laugh about in coming up with names to describe my altered appearance. I won't bother to repeat them. I didn't see anything humorous in any of it — all it did was remind me of how far from handsome I must appear to Miss Lyla Case. One thing I'll say about Cooper, the fact that nobody else thinks he's funny has never kept him from laughing long and hard at his own jokes.

I was glad when he finally left because I wanted to be alone to think about some things, mostly about Teacher. I had been trying to put some things together, like why he was here in Kecking Horse at all. He wasn't a teacher proper; I was willing to bet a month's store wages on that. He was educated all right, well-educated probably, and he'd been a lawman once which didn't surprise me at all. But none of that got me any closer to figuring out what he was doing in one of the sleepiest towns in all of Montana.

Anyway, things got busy in the store and then Cooper came back not long after, so I didn't get a lot more thinking done.

The population of Kecking Horse hadn't exactly exploded in all the time I'd been there. Somebody took a census once, I can't remember who did it or exactly when it was done, six or seven years before maybe, and the number had been one hundred and seventy-six souls. Funny isn't it that whenever anybody says the population of someplace, they always say 'souls'. I figure bodies would be a better word, one hundred and seventy-six bodies, but there must be some tradition about population counts and souls.

There had been some questions raised as to the accuracy of the Kecking Horse count, some claiming it included families who farmed or ranched outside of town and even a few that were likely nearer to other towns. Whatever the actual number was, I'm pretty sure it didn't grow by a whole lot in the nineties. You could pretty well bank on a death or two a year, sometimes five or six in a bad year with blizzards and such. Of course, there was the occasional baby born but that was barely enough to offset the decrease. For reasons I never got figured out, the supply of new babies in Kecking Horse was closer to a trickle than a flood. I don't know whether there was some problem between the men and women of the region and I wouldn't care to discuss it here if there was, but I can say that Joanna Bellingham, who did most of the midwifing for the town, had a lot of spare time on her hands.

There also wasn't a big migration into the area, at least not right where we were. So, it's understandable that folks viewed the arrival of three newcomers in not much more than a month as something close to a boom. Of course, I'm referring to Teacher, Virgil Watts and Miss Lyla Case. There were others who came and went during that time, but I see no reason to account for gamblers and gunfighters who aren't exactly citizens of a place anyway.

Not everyone was pleased with the sudden influx of souls. Some of the town's residents were worried that the population was rising at a rate they considered out of control. Cooper Raine looked at me one day over his coffee cup and muttered, "Where will it all end?"

So, it was a day of high historical importance, when on October the third, 1896, three more people climbed down from the stage and all of them stayed. The first of them, like most new arrivals, made the store his first stop. His name was Toots Parenteau. As soon as he was inside with the door closed behind him, he announced he was a cook and looking for work in the restaurant business. His timing was excellent because only a few weeks earlier Willie Sanburn, the previous cook over at the Independent Cities Hotel, died. Some said he died of poisoning after mistakenly eating some of his own cooking which, if it were true, was hardly a fitting way for a cook to become deceased. Eventually it came out that it was a Copperhead bite that took Willie, but by then the damage to his reputation had been done.

In the weeks since Willie's death, Cooper Raine had been filling in as cook in the restaurant when he wasn't busy with his other duties. As I've explained, not being busy was what Cooper was best at. His schedule didn't get any busier with the added chores because during the time he was employed as cook, the total number of customers that ate in the restaurant was four, and that included Jed Mead twice. Jed is eighty-eight and his mind's been gone for a dozen years or so. As bad as Willie Sanburn's cooking might have been, what he put on your plate was at least recognizable as food. The same couldn't be said for Cooper's creations, which would account for the slowness of business after he took over.

So, Toots' arrival was greeted with considerable good cheer all over town. He was quickly able to establish himself as a better cook than Cooper although that is a claim almost everybody in Montana could have safely made. While Toots didn't talk near as much as Cooper, he did talk just as loud and a lot of the things he said were just as crazy. But there was one other thing about Toots that stood him apart from Cooper and just about everybody else in Kecking Horse too. He was probably the toughest man in a fist-fight I ever saw. It soon got around that Toots had spent a lot of time up in Canada and had added considerably to his cooking income by fighting for money. After a while nobody would fight with him, not even the French-Canadian trappers who were supposed to be very tough men themselves. Some folks thought Watts should fight him seeing as he had experience in those slave boxing matches but Watts said that the only fighting he did anymore was with people he didn't like. Which made sense to me although there were those who thought him cowardly.

I mentioned there were three people on the stage that day. The other two skipped the stop at the store so I didn't find out much about them until sometime later. Cooper Raine dropped by to tell me their names were Cox and Hillier and that they were the newest employees of J. Emerson Keymore.

"I'd say old Keymore seems bent on hiring himself most of the cowhands in the territory," Cooper said, "which is hard to figure since he hasn't bought any more land and his herd ain't any bigger."

Cooper had a point, but I never liked to let him know that because it could keep him talking for several hours as he repeated that point over and over. So, I didn't say anything.

"And all of 'em look like they'd be just as at home in a gunfight as they would punchin' cows," he said. Which, it turned out, was another pretty good point.

A few things changed with Toots Parenteau's arrival in town. For one thing, people started eating at the restaurant again. In fact, there were evenings when it was downright busy in there with upwards of ten or twelve people at a time working on steaks and potatoes.

But the bigger news was the prize fight. As soon as word of Toots' abilities with his fists got around — and the local toughs got tired of being whipped — Cooper Raine recruited the help of Jake Martel, the implement man, and a couple of gamblers who'd been hanging around town for a few weeks to help organize the event. One of the gamblers, who said his name was Smith, had lived in Denver for a time and said he knew a couple of prize fighters there.

Telegrams were exchanged and the fight was set for a couple of weeks off: Terrible Toots Parenteau vs. Jim (Kid) Black. The "Terrible" and "Kid" were created by Cooper Raine who figured the two fighters' regular names weren't colourful enough. The fight was billed as the Montana Heavyweight Championship of the World, a name that never did make a lot of sense to me.

For one thing, the 'championship' part might have been a little far fetched, since none of the organizers of the fight bothered to find out if there were any other prize fighters in Montana, champions or otherwise. The same could be said for calling the fight a 'heavyweight' contest since Toots weighed no more than one hundred and seventy pounds with all his clothes on and nobody knew the weight of Kid Black. The gambler who arranged for his participation could recall only that "he's a big son of a bitch."

The fight soon grew into something much larger than a mere sporting exhibition. Marcus Warren decided that the official opening of the new school would be held the same day as the fight and Toots announced that at noon on the day of the match he would cook ham and eggs for everybody who cared to show up, on a giant outdoor cook stove he was building just for the occasion. He made a deal with the 40 Ranch to butcher three fat hogs (I figured Toots must have had some money saved up from his prize fights) and got the eggs donated from several small ranches in the area. And he wouldn't charge for his services as cook, either. When it was pointed out that the giant picnic would be taking place only a couple of hours before his scheduled prize fight, and might not be the best way of preparing for the bout, Toots said only, "Hell, boys, I'm only gonna cook the stuff. It ain't like I'm gonna eat it all."

I know it hasn't got much to do with what I was previously discussing, but it was right around that same period of time that I began to realize Miss Lyla Case would never return the feelings I had for her (and which were growing with each of my mother's fried chicken dinners). The reason was mountain stream clear to me. Miss Lyla Case had set her sights on Teacher. And who could blame her? I had long suspected this might be the case, but it was my first haircut in over a year that convinced me of it for certain.

I don't like having my hair cut — never have, particularly as Cooper Raine is the only barber from here to Great Falls and having to listen to Cooper talk for the three quarters of an hour it takes him to cut hair — he likes to work slow so he can get more said — is right alongside of drowning kittens for things I least like to do. I don't have to drown kittens anymore since we moved to town, but I still have to have haircuts.

So, when Miss Lyla Case informed me that she had cut gentlemen's hair from time to time, I asked her if she'd favour me with a trim. That very evening we were set up in the kitchen. Mother was upstairs, as she often was, sitting by her window and keeping an eye on Nettie Whitman's house for signs of suspicious behaviour. That meant Miss Lyla Case and I had the lower floor to ourselves. She told me to remove my shirt which, of course, I could not do in a house where ladies were present, but I did roll up my sleeves and let her fold my collar under. As she worked the scissors, we talked. Conversation with Miss Lyla Case was much more satisfying than it was with Cooper Raine.

"How long have you lived here?" she asked me.

"All my life," I answered. "Course we were out on a little ranch before we came to town." I figured she'd probably heard about Pa being killed so I didn't bother telling her that part.

"It's beautiful here," she said. "Does this valley have a name?"

"Yes, ma'am," I said, "they call it the Indian Head. Way off to the west, those are the Rocky Mountains."

"It is beautiful," she said again.

"If you like, I could take you for a ride down the valley some Sunday afternoon. It's even prettier a few miles south and west of here."

"I'd like that," she said. "I'm not much of a rider but I would like to do that."

"I can find a quiet horse for you, or maybe we could take Mr. Westover's buckboard. It's a pretty good road and there's lots to see."

"How ... how well do you know ... the other school teacher?" she asked. I noticed she didn't call him Teacher the way the rest of us did, like it was his name.

"Well ... I guess I ... I guess nobody knows him real well."

"He's not a real teacher, is he?"

"Well ...." I tried to think of what to say. I wanted to be truthful. "I can't say for sure." That was more or less true. He hadn't said he wasn't a teacher even when I'd asked him straight out. All he'd said was those references he'd sent when he applied for the job were false. And he hadn't even said that, exactly. Just sort of let on that they were. So, I guess my answer to Miss Lyla Case was pretty much the truth as I knew it.

"Anything else about him?" she said. "I mean I don't wish to pry into his private life, but he…is a different sort of man, don't you agree?"

"Different in what way, ma'am?"

"Well, different for a school teacher for starters, but more than that…he's not like most men."

"Yes," I nodded, just a small nod so's the hair wouldn't go down my neck. "I would say you're right."

"Do you like him?" she asked me.

"Yes, ma'am, I like him fine."

"I like him fine, too," she said.

I couldn't see her face since she was behind me working the scissors but there was something in her voice just then as she said 'I like him fine too' that made me understand I could never be any closer to her than I was at that moment while she was cutting my hair.

Naturally, Cooper Raine was wild when he saw my hair.

"Who ... who did that?" he yelled at me on the steps outside the store.

"If you mean who cut my hair, then the answer is Miss Lyla Case," I told him. "And she didn't talk my ear off the way you do."

"You oughta consider yourself damn lucky she didn't *cut* your ear off, the way she chopped away at your head." He circled around me and pointed the whole time. "I've seen chickens that's been plucked and still had more dignity than your head does right at this minute."

I'd never hit anybody up to that time (I'd tried the night I got jumped but that doesn't count since I'm pretty sure I missed with every swing) and wasn't sure how to go about it or I think I would have punched Cooper right there on the steps. It wasn't that I minded him making fun of the appearance of my scalp, but when he attacked the haircut itself, it seemed to me he was also insulting the person who did the cutting. And that angered me.

I didn't hit him though. Instead I stepped around him, trying hard to look like Teacher had when he'd stepped around Cook and Waincastle that day in the bar.

"Make you a wager," Cooper said just as I got to the door of the store.

I turned around and looked at him. "What kind of wager?"

"I'll bet you two dollars that with hair like that you won't get a single gal to dance with you."

I'd forgotten about the dance. That was the latest of the festivities that had been added to the day (and now night) of the prize fight. The schedule looked like this:

Morning   Official opening of the school
Noon   Toots' outdoor barbecue
Afternoon   The fight
Evening   The dance

The dance was scheduled to take place on an outdoor wooden floor to be built next to the

Independent Cities Hotel especially for the occasion. As I think about it now, it was a pretty smart bet for Cooper to make. I'd been to four dances in my life and had never succeeded in dancing with anybody, mostly because I'd yet to work up the courage to ask. I'd even tried going to a Sadie Hawkins dance once thinking that I might have better success if I didn't have to do the asking but things didn't turn out any better. So, I knew the chances of me doing any dancing were the other side of slim. But I felt strongly that I couldn't let the haircutting talents of Miss Lyla Case go undefended.

"It's a bet," I said and wheeled and went into the store.

I no sooner got inside the door than I remembered my broken nose. If a man can't get a dance partner when all his face parts are aimed in the direction they're supposed to be, what chance does he have with a nose that has more bends in it than a garter snake on a hot rock.

I must have said that out loud because Mr. Westover who was inside the store as I came in laughed out loud. "Maybe there'll be someone at that dance that likes crooked honkers. I hear it's all the rage out in California. Men are rushing out and getting their noses busted just so they can be popular with beautiful women."

I didn't believe him, of course, though Mr. Westover isn't normally much for joking. And if it was a joke, I didn't see anything very funny about it.

We'd had one more work bee before the official opening of the school. And though there was still finishing work to do, and the students wouldn't actually be in the school for another week, that didn't dampen the enthusiasm of Mr. Marcus Warren or any of the people, I judged there to be fifty or sixty, who showed up for the event.

I won't bore you with the contents of the speech — they bored me about to death — but I will say I didn't think much of what was in it. I thought a lot about what wasn't in it though. Not a word was said about all the work Teacher had done on his own or the fact he had been guarding the school all this time. Several people complained to each other and said we ought to thank Teacher publicly. But nobody took up the matter with Mr. Warren and as far as I know, no one said anything to Teacher.

We rode back to Kecking Horse as a group and I spent most of the time surveying possible dance partners. By the time we got to town, I was feeling mightily depressed. I was sure none of the town's single ladies — and there weren't all that many of them — would care to be seen with someone whose nose was being immortalized in the poems of Cooper Raine. Stupid poems at that but which he was busy reciting anywhere a group of people happened to gather. To Cooper, a 'group' consisted of himself and at least one other person.

We arrived back on Main Street about the time Toots' barbecue was getting rolling. People were loading up plates with eggs and big slices of ham, and Toots, true to his word, was dressed in a white apron-looking thing and flipping meat on the giant grill he had constructed. I rode home and gathered up Mother. You get some idea of the importance of the event when you realize she was making one of her rare excursions out of the house to sample Toots' outdoor cooking skills.

The ham and eggs turned out very well although the eating was made less enjoyable by a sudden downpour that sent us all scattering for cover. Mother and I wound up with Virgil Watts and Archie Cuddy on the end of a wagon we rolled under an overhang on the east side of the livery. Mother didn't complain much. In fact, Virgil Watts and her, they got into a real interesting discussion about the breaking of bad horses. I jumped into the chat myself along about the time they got to discussing Prince and the challenge he had been to break. You remember that Prince had been Archie's horse and I'm pleased to say the conversation appeared to put him right off his food.

At one point, as Watts was going on about the need to win a horse's trust (Mother was nodding and saying 'absolutely' a lot), Archie must have been feeling a touch uncomfortable.

Finally Archie must have felt the need to break the silence. "Of course, you'd never have broke that horse if I hadn't already done some real good work on the basics — sort of got him ready to be broke." When Archie said that he didn't give out a hint of a smile or anything. He actually wanted us to believe him.

"What work was that, Mr. Cuddy?" Watts asked, all innocent like.

"Well ... you know ... handling the horse, halter breaking him, yep, I gave him a good start all right. Would have done even more if it wasn't for this damn arthritis, pardon my language Ma'am."

I looked at Watts. I didn't think he'd ever say a hard word to anybody, not even a liar like Archie Cuddy. And I was right. Then I looked over at Mother. I suspected she wouldn't be nearly so reluctant about expressing her opinion. I was right again.

"From what I've heard, Mr. Cuddy," she said, "the first man to lay a hand on that horse since he was gelded as a yearling, was this gentleman, and it's a good thing too because the horse might've killed you or anybody else that tried to handle him, arthritis or no arthritis."

I could see Archie was mighty upset with the tone of Mother's remarks, but I guess he felt that arguing with a widow about horses that could kill folks was unseemly. So, he didn't. He didn't eat his dinner neither. Just sat and watched the rain run off the edge of that overhang. I felt he had some kind of reckoning coming to him for sticking Watts with the rankest horse in the country, but at least he hadn't *sold* him the horse, which would have made it worse. Mother seemed to enjoy the conversation and I did too. We polished off our dinners like they were our last meal.

The rain quit about fifteen minutes before the prizefight was scheduled to begin. You may not be surprised to learn that nowhere in the town of Kecking Horse did a regulation prizefight ring exist. Cooper Raine had sent off letters (Miss Lyla Case helped with the composing) to Missoula and Great Falls but was unable to come up with a ring. I suggested that he make one, but I realized after I said it that it was a foolish suggestion since building a ring would have involved work on Cooper's part.

He had, however, come up with a solution. Or so he announced to everyone just about the time the last of the ham steaks were being removed from Toots' grill.

"What we are going to do," announced Cooper in a voice that could probably be heard clear to the Bar U, "is we are going to form a human ring. Men will link arms and form a circle around the combatants (he pronounced it combanitants). You will not only have a ringside view. You will be the ringside its very self."

Then Cooper called for volunteers. The response was ... well, it was slow. You see, there were a couple of problems with Cooper's plan. One was that a lot of the men had not only eaten, they had washed down their dinners with various refreshments. And the majority of these men would have had a difficult time standing in a circle, or any other shape, even with their arms linked. The second problem was that of the men who would have been able to form and maintain a ring (it would have been a very small ring), none of them was interested in standing arm to arm because what they wanted to do was to place bets on the fight as it went along. You couldn't do that if you were part of the fight facility.

When Cooper called for volunteers, only two people stepped forward. Archie Cuddy. And me. I figured Archie was still in a bad mood from dinner and thought with any luck he might be able to take a poke at one of the combanitants. Me? Well, I volunteer for everything, which is stupid, I know, but I feel obliged to. But after I'd stepped forward and saw that there were only two volunteers and also recalled Cooper's rudeness on the subject of Miss Lyla Case's haircutting abilities, I turned around and stepped back.

The Montana Heavyweight Championship of the World began as a ringless fight. Which is probably the only reason it lasted as long as it did. Kid Black was almost a head taller than Toots, maybe one and a half times as thick and one of the meanest looking men I'd ever seen. Problem was he wasn't much tougher than a fresh tea biscuit. What he was though, was fast. Which probably accounted for the fact he had survived this long as a prizefighter. Thanks to Cooper's oversight on the ring question, Kid Black had most of Kecking Horse to run around in while trying to avoid Toots' fists. The fight had been going on for the better part of a half hour and no blows had been struck. Kid Black hopped, jumped, skipped and, a lot of the time, just plain ran around every square inch of Main Street to keep out of Toots' way. The rain that had fallen before the fight had cooled the air to the point where it looked like the Denver Invader (as Cooper had called him in the introduction of the fighters) might be able to keep running for a very long time. Terrible Toots in the meantime, just kept stalking after Kid Black and muttering, "Son of a bitch." None of us were sure if Toots was directing the remark at his opponent or if it was just a general commentary on the whole situation. A lot of the spectators were also directing comments toward the Denver Invader and most of them were much less hospitable than what had come out of Toots.

It became obvious something had to be done or the bout wouldn't be completed in time for the dance and maybe not even for spring seeding. An interesting thing happened. Men, who minutes before had been pacing up and down the street to catch a glimpse of the uneventful proceedings or leaning against buildings having a smoke and a drink straightened themselves up, exchanged a look here or there and began to link up arms.

The gambling crowd, having put all the money on Toots that the house would take by ten minutes into the fight, joined in the miraculous formation of a ring. As this was happening (I linked up with Watts and Jake Martel), Cooper kept yelling, "That's it, Gentlemen, that's it." Toots' repetitions of "Son of a bitch" became more frequent, and I may have imagined this, but I'm quite sure I heard Kid Black say "Oh, Shit."

Once the ring was fully formed, the prize fight didn't last long. I will say that Kid Black, once he was forced to, fought hard and with a certain behind-the-barn desperation. However, as I have mentioned, Kid Black's main defects were that he was neither tough nor good at fighting. Toots, of course, was both. On top of which, he was somewhat grumpy from having traipsed through the mud on Main Street for a very long time trying to get close enough to his opponent to actually fight.

When he did, with the help of a ring that got smaller and smaller, the battle, as I mentioned, was brief. Kid Black tried, which surprised many of us, but he didn't like to be hit. Especially, he didn't like to be hit by someone like Toots who could hit very hard and very often. When the fight was over, there were several arguments — some lasted for months — about how many times Kid Black was able to get back up after being knocked down. Most agreed that it was three times, though I recollected only two myself and, of course, Cooper swore it was five times that "the Denver Invader courageously rose to face his foe."

Eventually, Kid Black did not rise, courageously or any other way, and his foe was loudly proclaimed to be "The Montana Heavyweight Champion of the World", which I still think was a silly thing to call him.

When the fight was over, I went looking for Teacher. To be completely honest, I was going to offer to spell him off and stand guard at the school that night, which, of course, would have saved me the humiliation of going to the dance and not having a single dance partner the entire evening. (And two dollars as well). I never found him though — and I realized I hadn't seen him since the school opening. I wasn't sure why he hadn't come to the fight, but I was certain that he hadn't ridden into the hills to brood on Judge Marcus Warren's slight. It was more likely he just didn't enjoy watching prize fighting or possibly he felt he should be especially careful about guarding the school on a day when most everybody's attention was elsewhere.

Anyway, I didn't find him. Which meant I had no reason not to take my broken nose to the dance and lose the bet with Cooper Raine. I looked up both Watts and Miss Lyla Case and neither of them knew where Teacher was. I have to admit I was kind of relieved that Miss Lyla Case was still in town. Had she and Teacher both been missing, I wouldn't have known what to think.

I went home between the prize fight and the dance to help Mother with a few chores and clean up. I was to learn that Mother had not only stayed for the fight but had taken a dollar from

Nettie Whitman in a wager. She was very pleased about that.

It was time to make my garment selection. Not that there was that much choice. It boiled down to deciding between my blue shirt and brown wool trousers or my black suit. The necktie, also black, would be the same in either case, since I only had one. Much as I disliked the itchy wool of the brown trousers, I generally wore the black suit for church, weddings and funerals and felt that maybe it was a touch formal for a dance (no doubt Cooper would have had something to say about the similarity between what was going to happen to me that night and funerals, but I didn't give that a lot of thought just then).

I might have chosen the more solemn attire had I known that my life would change forever at that dance. Seems like a man ought to be formally dressed for life-altering occasions. But, at the time I was getting myself ready for the dance, I had no idea that the combination of Floyd Martel and Sarah-Beth Hutt were going to have such an impact on my future.

Chapter Eight

So, I decided on the blue shirt and brown wool trousers. I reasoned that since it was unlikely I'd be doing much moving around (as in dancing), the itch wouldn't be all that bad. I even patted some toilet water on my face. I'd found it after Teacher moved out of the house and, well, to tell the truth, I hadn't bothered to mention it to him. I figured he probably had more anyway. It was the first experience my face had ever had with toilet water, but I don't think that had much to do with what happened later. Besides, how could Sarah-Beth Hutt have smelled my face from way across the dance floor? Especially with the dance floor being situated right next to the livery, which had its own set of smells, much more powerful than the toilet water I'd ladled fairly generously onto cheeks and chin.

The dance was to take place on a makeshift plank floor set next to the Independent Cities Hotel. It was set there for the convenience of the men who had to walk only a few steps to be at the hotel's bar where Jake Drury had the foresight to lay in a large quantity of liquor for the day. Chairs were recruited from the hotel, the town's businesses and even private homes and were placed around the perimeter of the floor to allow the ladies and some of the older gentlemen to sit. Most of the younger men stood — drinking, smoking and sizing up the occupants of the chairs.

Lots of us had heard that Floyd Martel was a handy man with a fiddle, but because Mr. Westover had always arranged the dances and wasn't about to hire his rival businessman to provide the music, nobody knew for sure. But this dance hadn't been organized by Mr. Westover and as soon as I arrived, I knew this would be an event with a difference. For one thing, Cooper Raine and his mouth organ weren't front and centre and Nettie Whitman wouldn't be nose-singing either. That was important. Nettie herself didn't call what she did nose-singing; it was a name given to it by others. You see, Nettie did sing, all right, but she generally forgot about three-quarters of the words, even of her favourite songs, and when she did that, she'd go to making an open-mouthed, teeth-clenched humming sort of noise that set strong men's eyes to watering and vicious dogs to whining something unmerciful. Seeing Floyd Martel up there putting some kind of stuff on his bow strings meant there'd be no mouth organ, no nose-singing and a lot less whining. I figured even if I lost the bet, at least the evening would be more tolerably spent than many.

It got better. One of the reasons I never had a lot of dance partners was that I don't actually ask women to dance with me. My practice instead had been to pick one out and stare hard at her hoping that somehow she would figure out I wanted to dance with her. This method has never worked but I always found it preferable to actually walking across what feels like several miles of barbed wire and badger holes to ask somebody to dance with me. Especially since on those occasions when I had tried it—I was much younger then—the woman I asked would turn to me with an 'oh-my-God-not-him' look on her face, say no thanks and turn away to examine worn spots on the wall. The walk that goes before the askin' is nothing compared to the walk back, toward the grinning faces of the other young men, most of whom had by then spent a least *some* time on the dance floor moving here and there like Kingfishers protecting their eggs. And, of course, there was Cooper Raine's voice, louder than the worst of the whining dogs, saying things like, "Turned down again, eh? Better luck next time."

That had been the pattern before the broken nose. So, I knew asking someone to dance in my post nose-break period was out of the question unless I was hankering for a large helping of humiliation. Which I wasn't. I decided to go back to the stare-and-hope method. For the first hour, the results were what they had always been. Even with the improved quality of the music, I had willed not one female to rise from her seat and float over to me, hand extended. Cooper Raine had been a dancing fool all night

— he'd even twirled Miss Lyla Case a couple of times — which made me wish that lightning would strike him dead. Each time Cooper passed me he reminded me of our bet and had taken to calling me names, silly ones like Twinkle Toes and Magic Shoes, the kind of thing you'd expect from Cooper.

I will remember the moment all my life. I was staring up at the sky thinking about stars and how fine it would be to live on one, when I felt a tap on my shoulder. I turned around, ready to tell Cooper to shut his darn mouth. I didn't get a chance to say it though because Sarah-Beth Hutt was standing where I had expected Cooper to be. And she was smiling.

"Feel like dancing, William?" she said.

I blinked at her. Then I swallowed. Out of the blue, the wool trousers that hadn't itched all night began attacking my legs like an Old Testament plague. I wanted to scratch but, of course, I couldn't, and I'm pretty sure I was sweating. So, I blinked and swallowed and itched and sweated all at once.

"Uh ... dance?" I said.

"Yes, you know ... out there ... shuffle, shuffle to the music. "

"Yeah, that's right," I said. I've never been sure why Sarah-Beth didn't just turn away and ask someone slightly less stupid to dance.

But she didn't. Instead she smiled and reached out and took my hand. "Come on," she said.

I followed her to the dance floor. I had a bit of a feeling this wasn't how it was supposed to happen — that I should be leading Sarah-Beth to the dance floor, not following her. I was also pretty sure I could hear snickers from behind me. I didn't much care though because I was about to dance with a girl for the first time in my life *and* win two dollars from Cooper Raine.

I felt duty-bound to give Sarah-Beth an opportunity to reconsider. "Are you sure you don't mind, I mean, dancing with me, what with my nose and all?"

She looked at me and I noticed that although Sarah-Beth couldn't be called pretty in the way Miss Lyla Case was pretty, there was something very nice about her face, especially the little smile that was there a lot of the time.

"Does your nose have anything to do with how you move your feet?" She was smiling the smile I just told you about when she asked me, but she wasn't laughing at me. At least I didn't think she was.

"What?" I said. I knew I hadn't said a single intelligent thing to Sarah-Beth so far and I was wishing I could, but it seemed impossible. I talked to women all the time in the store but discussing curtains and tablecloths across a counter is very different from talking about anything at all on a dance floor.

"As long as you don't step on my feet, everything will be fine," Sarah-Beth said, "and I'm sure your nose won't cause you to do that."

"No, probably not," I said. "I guess I was thinking more about how I look."

"You look very nice," Sarah-Beth said to me in this soft voice that made me think she meant it.

We were going by Cooper. His mouth was open. I grinned at him so hard my eyes wrinkled shut.

"Sorry I can't talk to you, Cooper," I said. "I'm going dancing just now." Darn, I enjoyed saying that.

Just about then a real bad thought slipped its way into my mind. What if I didn't know how to dance? I mean there was a real good chance of that since I'd never actually done it. About the time I was starting to feel mighty panicky about the situation, Floyd started playing.

As I've already explained, Floyd played very well. It was *what* he was playing that was a problem. Floyd chose that moment to play the slowest song he'd played all night. Which meant that I was going to have to get up kind of close to Sarah-Beth. And even though I've already told you about Julie, you have to realize I'd never touched a woman with a whole bunch of people watching. I'd also never realized just how complicated a thing dancing was. Sarah-Beth was a fair bit shorter than me and she was looking up at me as she stepped toward me. Actually, she moved right up against me. When she did that the pants-itch became plumb unbelievable. I took a step backward.

My first few attempts to get my hands in their proper places must have had a fair resemblance to the not-quite-punches Kid Black sent in the general direction of Toots Parenteau. Most of them hadn't ended up in the right places either. The snickering was getting louder behind me. It was becoming clear I had to do something more or less definite. I aimed my left hand at Sarah-Beth's waist, reached out and struck her, not hard mind you, pretty well in the middle of her bosom. I guess that's when Sarah-Beth thought she better help me. She got my hands where they belonged. By this time, the noise behind me wasn't snickering anymore. It was ... well, it was more than that. And some of the fellas were making comments too, comments which don't require repeating here.

What saved me was my feet. For some reason, they were able to do what my brain, my mouth, and for sure my hands, were not. They were able to conduct themselves with dignity when standing opposite Sarah-Beth Hutt. And something else. They were able to dance.

I'm not sure why. The pants were itching, and I think I'd sweated enough to drown a fair-sized chicken, but my feet didn't care about any of that. They figured out on their own how to move to music without hurting the person in the next shoes. And Sarah-Beth Hutt and I danced. Not just once, mind you. And not just to slow songs neither.

Now you may not believe what I'm about to tell you, but after those first few experiences with Sarah-Beth Hutt, it was like I'd been on dance floors all my life. I danced with lots of women — I even asked most of them — and near the end of the evening, I danced with Miss Lyla Case, although I have to admit my pants broke into itching again for that part. I danced the last two songs of the night with Sarah-Beth. They were both slow dances and I guess she must have liked my dancing pretty much and not been too put off by my nose either, because during those last dances she got so close to me her bosom was pressed right up against me. Maybe she thought that was the best way to keep it from being run into, I don't know. What I do know is that it felt very nice to dance with her that way.

I guess it was all the dancing and everything and winning the bet with Cooper Raine and having Sarah-Beth up real close to me that made me completely forget to notice Teacher still wasn't around. The dance was ending, and I saw Watts talking to Miss Lyla Case and that's when I realized Teacher hadn't been around since the morning's ceremony out at the school. We were standing there talking about it — Sarah-Beth was standing with me — when we heard horses coming slowly toward us from out of the shadows.

When they got closer, I could see that there was only one rider. It was Teacher and he was leading another horse. There was someone on the other horse, but he wasn't riding. He was slung over the saddle and tied on. You could tell right away that whoever it was laying over his saddle like that was dead. Teacher rode by our little group and stopped his horse in front of Mr. Marcus Warren, who you will recall is a judge and the closest thing we have to a representative of the legal system in these parts. I could hear Teacher speaking to him.

"The man back there," he indicated with his thumb, "tried to burn down the school this evening. When I suggested he shouldn't do that, he pulled his gun and I was forced to kill him. There were no witnesses, so it'll be a case of his word against mine and he isn't saying much. You do whatever you feel like, Judge..." he raised his voice then and spoke to everybody there, "but I want people to know that anybody who tries to do harm to the school or to anyone connected with it, or with me, will end up the same way as the man on that horse."

Then he reached down and handed the lead shank of the second horse to Mr. Warren, turned and rode back into the shadows. I walked over to where Mr. Warren was holding the horse and looking very uncomfortable. Maybe he didn't think it was fitting that on the very day the new school was dedicated, one of the teachers should shoot somebody. I admit I'd gone over there to see who was strapped to that horse. I didn't know the man, but Cooper Raine told us it was Nate Gillis, one of J. Emerson Keymore's new hands.

It had been a very full day for a place the size of Kecking Horse. A lot of history was made in the town that day. And as I stood there looking at the dead man tied onto the back of that bay horse, I had a feeling there'd be a lot more made in the days ahead. I didn't think about it all that long though, as right then Sarah-Beth asked me if I'd be kind enough to escort her home. And I did.

Chapter Nine

Things were quiet for a spell after that except for the running of Kid Black out of town. After the fight, it turned out the Denver Invader took a liking to life in Kecking Horse. Story was it was a sporting lady named Jane and a good run of luck at stud poker that made him feel at home in our community.

But when the word got out that the Kid himself had been betting on Toots to win the fight, things became a whole lot less hospitable. A number of citizens had bet a considerable amount of their savings on Kid Black — I guess they felt that anybody who'd come that far to fight must be pretty good at it — and they turned unfriendly when they learned the Kid had been investing in Toots. Turns out he'd even borrowed wagering capital from a couple of people in exchange for a piece of advice. The advice, it turned out, was to bet on the other guy — that being Toots.

Next thing we knew a good-sized mob had organized itself and was looking for Kid Black. It was only the second time I could recall a mob forming up in Kecking Horse. The first time was back in '89 when word got out that an old Chinese who ran a laundry out of a tent behind

Main Street had come down with smallpox. His name was Kim High-Wo and he'd gone up to Calgary to visit his brother. There was smallpox there and old High-Wo got it and brought it back with him. I wasn't real proud of the way some of my neighbours behaved on that occasion. They burned the laundry tent and everything in it — that part you could understand — but then they got hold of High-Wo and cut off his pigtails and ran him out of town even though he was so sick he could barely sit a horse. I never heard what happened to him after that, but I don't imagine it was good.

This time the mob didn't catch up to its prey. Kid Black got wind of what was happening, gathered up his winnings and rode out of town on the horse that brought in the body of Nate Gillis. The talk for the next few days was about whether taking a dead man's horse amounted to stealing which would have required a posse being formed to go get Kid Black and bring him back. Most figured it didn't.

After that, we got our first storm of the season, much earlier than usual, and everybody was forced to hunker down for several days, so I didn't see many people. The snow piled up in drifts in front of the store, which meant that about the only person who came around during that time was Cooper Raine. I'm sure an entire mountain of snow wouldn't have kept Cooper from irritating those he'd chosen to irritate. So, for four days I opened up the store — Mr. Westover came in for an hour or so each day, then left — and I spent a lot of time listening to Cooper discuss things he knew nothing about.

Mostly he talked about Teacher. "He shot that man dead," he said. Cooper had always been good at stating the obvious.

"Yes, he did," I said.

"I think he should be arrested for that, maybe hung," Cooper was blowing on his fourth or fifth cup of coffee as he said that.

"Why?" I asked him.

"You don't believe that story about how the man was fixin' to blow up the school, do you?"

"Burn down."

"What?"

"He wasn't going to blow up the school," I said. "He was going to burn it down."

"That's what Teacher says."

"That's what he says, all right," I said.

"Well, I don't believe it."

"Probably the best thing you could do, in that case, is to go see Mr. Marcus Warren and have yourself deputized, then ride out there and arrest him."

Cooper thought about that. Thought about it for quite a long time.

"And another thing," he said, "it's a terrible thing what he's teaching those kids."

"Oh?" I wondered if he'd got wind of the outdoors days or the threat to burst kids into flames if they misbehaved.

"Yep," Cooper said. "He's got them reading a book called *The Scarlet Letter*. It's typical of them books by them Easterners. There's a woman in there who sins with a man she ain't married to — a Reverend, no less — and then the book makes it sound like her and the Reverend are the only good people in the whole community. Sinful's what it is, teachin' something like that to kids."

Now, one thing I was pretty sure of was that Cooper Raine hadn't consumed a whole bunch of books during his life.

"You read this book, this *Scarlet Letter*?" I asked him.

"Hell, no," he shouted. "I'm not about to partake in the devil's readings. But I was told about it. I've a good mind to get some people together and have it stopped."

"Have what stopped?"

"The readin' of sinful practices like that." He waved his coffee cup around and some coffee spilled out. "Out at that school. Bet I could get up a committee and we could put a stop to it. Get that book right out of that school."

"Imagine you could, all right," I said. "There's probably lots of people around who also haven't read the book and would like to be on your committee."

Sarcasm is something that's pretty much wasted on a man like Cooper Raine. When I said that about the committee, he just nodded his head and took a sip of the coffee.

"Probably be a whole lot easier than arresting Teacher, too," I said.

"Oh, I could arrest him, all right," Cooper said. "Yessir, I'm just the man to handle that job if it should come to that."

"Well, if you decide to go arrest him, let me know," I said. "I'll go along with you. I can lead you and your horse back to town afterward. Save Teacher another trip."

It took a minute, but Cooper eventually figured out what I meant.

"I reckon you cheated," he said.

"What?"

"I figure you paid off that Hutt gal to dance with you. Maybe offered her half the winnings."

It was one of Cooper's favourite tricks. Whenever he was in danger of losing an argument, which wasn't often since most people left before the argument was concluded, he'd change the subject, like he was doing now.

"Well, I didn't pay her," I said. "And besides there haven't been any winnings since you haven't bothered to pay up yet."

Cooper sipped away at his coffee. "Yep, if there's arresting to be done, I'd be the fella to call on," he said.

You can understand why I was some happy when the weather broke and other people began coming into the store.

Chapter Ten

I haven't mentioned it before but the next part of the story I can't tell you, because I wasn't there. Of course, I *could* tell it, but then it would be more like history, which is often written by people who weren't actually around and are just hearing about it from somebody else. I could have written it like that, all right, just talked to Cal Chapin and got the story from him and then passed it along, *sort of* accurate, but not really.

But so far, except for Watts telling how he got jumped that night, everything I've written is about things I either did or saw. And even then, I wouldn't swear that I've got everything exactly right. It seems to me there's a whole lot between seeing something as it's happening and the passing it along to someone else. Maybe that's why I've never had a whole bunch of faith in what we read in the history books.

Take Nero, for instance. Everything I've ever read about him talks about how he murdered his mother and his sister and a bunch of other folks too and sat around playing his fiddle while the town was going up in flames. Thing is, every telling of Nero's life that I've ever read comes from some historian fella who wasn't actually there when the murdering and the burning were taking place. So that fella is just repeating what was heard from somebody else. There's a fancy word for that — research. Which might be fine and good, or it might not be.

What if the person who first wrote about Nero, what if that person didn't like the emperor, maybe had a run-in with him over a land deal or a wife or something? You can see how that person's telling of the story of Nero's life might have a little slant to it. Sort of the way my talking about Cooper Raine does if I'm not real careful. I have this feeling that a lot of the time history is more along the lines of *his-story*.

Anyway, I figured it would be better to have Cal tell this part of the thing himself so that you'd get a little truer version of it. And he will directly. But I should explain one or two things first.

What happened was somebody took some shots at Teacher. He figured there were two men who shot at him, though I'm not sure how he came to that conclusion since the shooting was done at night by someone who was hidden in some brush not far from the new school. It happened about a week after the storm ended and two weeks after Teacher killed Nate Gillis. He figured someone was trying to get even or at least scare him off. I could understand that all right, but I was mighty surprised when he up and resigned his position with the school and announced he was going after the men. They had lit out right after the shooting. Maybe they figured Teacher would be after them, I don't know.

Now the way Cal Chapin came into all this was through his little sister Rose who was one of the students at the school. She mentioned to Teacher her brother had been a tracker for the army and since Watts was up in the hills with a herd and couldn't be found, Teacher asked Cal if he'd care to go for a ride after the men.

Most of us figured that it was Cox and Hillier, the two new arrivals in town, who had done the shooting since they were the ones who suddenly got scarcer than winter gophers in the days right after. That's all I can tell you, so I'll leave the writing to Cal for the next while. He's a man with some education although he's not what you'd call a literate man. I hope you'll find him acceptable. I fixed up the spelling a little — I told him I'd do that when I asked him to write this part and he said that would be all right — but I left the way he says things pretty much alone. I figured if I changed that part, then it'd be me telling it instead of Cal. He also wanted to give his part its own title and I told him he could since he worked mighty hard at the writing.

I still recollect it pretty good, that trip with Teacher. When he come to me, I told him I ain't tracked nothin' since the spring of '90 when we went after an Indian who'd gutted a woman over to Nebraska after she'd shot him in the foot for stealin' one of her chickens.

Teacher said he didn't care if my experience was current or not, that's how he put it, as long as I could find the men who'd tried to gun him. I told him I could if anybody could, and the next morning, we was headin' north right into a wind that cut through our clothes like we wasn't wearin' any. I told him right off that if it storms there wouldn't be no sign and findin' those men would be as close to impossible as catchin' bass without no hook. But he said let's ride, we'll find them. So, we rode off into that wind.

I didn't think much about the danger part. I expect it was because Teacher said he'd handle the dealin's with the men when we found them and all I had to do was to get him close enough to do that. Me and Teacher, we'd never met before that even though my sister went to his school and all. But as soon as we set off to ridin'

I knew there was a lot more killer to the man than there was teacher. He was friendly enough all right, downright pleasant to me in fact and always polite to women and what not that we came onto while we was ridin. But I always knew there was a meanness inside there that would come out if it was needed.

First day out, I found sign that showed two men headed north. Teacher figured they'd make for them Northwest Territories up to the far end of Canada and hole up there for the winter. I didn't figure that was such a bad idea, probably would've done the same thing myself if I'd taken a few shots at someone who looked as handy at killin' as Teacher looked.

We didn't talk much, I ain't that inclined toward conversation, I figured if he'd wanted lots of talk, he would've invited along Cooper Raine, who's a mostly no account mouth-flood who lives in Kecking Horse. Teacher, he didn't have much to say neither; he seemed just to think a lot of the time. I don't know if he was thinkin' about whether to kill those boys or not, I doubt it because if you ask me, he probably had his mind made up about that already. So maybe he was thinkin' about what he'd do after they were killed now that he'd quit his school teachin' job. I figured three, four days we'd find them if the weather held up and then we'd be headed back. Turns out my calculation was off by considerable, partly because the weather didn't hold and partly for other reasons.

The first night we were on the trail we come to a little ranch house a ways this side of the Milk River. There was two women livin' in that ranch house, two of the damnedest women you ever saw in your life. I apologize for using the word damn right there alongside the word women, but I don't know another way to describe Hazel and Ef Burnside. At first, I thought they was mother and daughter with Ef being a bunch more elderly than Hazel, but they turned out to be sisters. They had been runnin' the place by theirselves ever since Ef ran her husband off, a man who took a greater shine to the drink than he did to workin'. So said Ef, leastways.

So, there they were, those two women, runnin' a ranch with better than a hundred head of cows and twenty or more horses. We got there about sundown, and Teacher, right off, he asks if the women have seen Cox and Hillier, the two fellas we was after. Ef, she did most of the talkin' most of the time, said, yeah they seen 'em. They stopped there for water for theirselves and their horses and asked about tradin' Hillier's horse for another since his was lame on a front leg. Ef said she agreed to trade if they'd throw in twenty dollars since the horse Hillier was gettin' was sound. Hillier took exception to that suggestion and after that, the two men went to drinkin' and suggested that maybe the ladies would have to earn that extra twenty dollars.

That turned out to be the wrong thing to say and Ef got the shotgun and Cox and Hillier rode out in a hurry. Later that night they snuck back and took the horse they wanted and left the lame one. The ladies seemed to be glad that we was lookin' for those two men.

"You're welcome to bed down in the barn," Ef told us, "but before you do that we'll cook you some chicken stew, if you like."

Teacher thanked the ladies real polite and told 'em we'd be proud to share a meal with 'em. Except we didn't share it exactly. Ef and Hazel had ate some time before so it was a matter of Teacher and me doin' the eatin' and the two ladies sittin' across from us, Ef mostly talkin', Hazel mostly watchin'. She was mostly watchin' Teacher. I can't say I was real comfortable eatin' away with them women lookin' on like that. I was never sure if my manners was right up to what they should be but I sneaked some looks at Teacher and picked up a few things about the handlin' of a knife and fork in ways they didn't generally get handled in our house. Course, I couldn't be sure that the way Teacher was doin' it was correct either, but the ladies seemed to approve of how we ate, and I ended up near foundered on chicken stew. When we was done eatin' Teacher told the ladies that we'd be leavin' at first light and thanked them again for the supper. Ef told us which direction Cox and Hillier had rode off and I figured our adventures at that little ranch house had about came to an end. Turns out I was wrong about that too.

The women must've salted that chicken stew a-plenty, and I drank considerable water before I laid down in that barn. The result of all the water drinkin' was that in the middle of the night I had to step outside. I figured privacy wasn't all that important since it was pitch dark and the house was quiet. So, I just stepped behind a decent sized bush and made my water, at the same time thinkin' 'bout how unseasonably warm it was. When I'd finished, I was havin' a little trouble with the buttons on my trousers in the dark and all when suddenly this voice, all soft and low and raspy says, "No need to do up them buttons."

I jumped straight up and right the way around all at the same time. Who's standin' there but Ef. I didn't know that right away, but I discovered it fast enough when she lit up a lantern and stood there lookin' at me with a smile on her face. I was so surprised that I sort of forgot I hadn't finished puttin' my ... self ... back into my pants. I was considerably more surprised when Ef suddenly reached down and took hold of my ... self.

This, I want you to know, is not something that had ever happened to me in the entire history of myself. I couldn't say anythin' and I was havin' a bad time with breathin' but the part of me that Ef was holdin' seemed to be doing fine — maybe as fine as it had ever done. And the next thing I knew, Ef had led me over behind a line of bushes that ran along the back and one side of the house and pulled me down behind them bushes. I can't in good Christian conscience describe to you what went on behind them bushes but I will admit that it was nigh on daylight before I got back to the barn.

Teacher was awake and pullin' on his boots. He looked at me and smiled. "Get a good rest, did you, Cal?" was all he said but I had a feelin' he knew what had been goin' on out there in the dark next to them bushes.

"No sir," I said to him, "that is, yes sir ... well, actually, no, sir, I went to relieve myself a while back and couldn't get back to sleep so I been walkin' around out there ... in the dark ... out in the field ... not near the house, you understand."

He just nodded, Teacher did. "Terrible thing, a restless night," he said. "Hope it doesn't affect your tracking abilities."

We saddled up and were on our horses, about to ride out when Ef and Hazel came out of the house. Hazel handed Teacher a bundle all bound up real nice in a tablecloth, it looked like.

"There's sandwiches in there," she said, and her eyes were on Teacher the same way they was the night before. I was wonderin' what might've happened if Teacher had stepped out of the barn to relieve *him*self during the night.

"Appreciate it Ma'am," Teacher touched his hat and reached down for the sandwiches.

"I expect I'll be seeing you again." Ef patted me on the leg.

I felt kind of embarrassed and looked over at Teacher but he didn't say anythin'. There's a couple of other things I should tell you, I guess. One is that Ef Burnside was not a beautiful woman, not even from far off. And a night without sleep in favour of what we'd been doin in its place didn't improve her appearance any. The other thing I had ought to mention is how the whole time Ef and me were on the ground back of them bushes, she never stopped talkin'.

At first most of the talk had to do with what we was doin' and how she'd appreciate it if I was to do such and such a thing. There was a lot of sighin' and moanin' too, some of it borderin' on yellin' and I was about half surprised that Teacher didn't come rushin' up, gun in hand, figurin' the woman was bein' killed.

Later on, she cut back on that sort of thing and went to straight conversation, a lot of it about how her and me was right suited to one another and ought to think about partnerin' up permanent. Not long before daylight, she started referrin' to us as an engaged couple. Now up to that time, I hadn't really participated much in the conversation, although earlier on I admit I did a little moanin' and groanin' myself, but when the word engaged came up — it came up quite a few times near the end there — it kind of got my attention, a bit like Dr. Bell's ointment on an open saddle sore. That's about when I separated myself from Ef and headed back to the barn hopin' that she'd kind of overlook the engagement situation once the light of mornin' hit and we was both back in our britches. But, from the way she patted my leg and kept winkin' her eye at me as I was gettin' set to ride off, I was pretty sure the idea of partnerin' permanent hadn't totally gone out of Ef's mind.

"The Milk River's a couple a days ride north," she said to Teacher. "I expect you men will end up there. River's high we've heard, so don't drown. And send this one here back when you've done with him." She looked at me and then she looked at Hazel before she went on talkin' to Teacher.

"'Spect we'd have a place for you here as well if you'd care to stop by for a few years," she said and she patted my leg again even though the invitation was to Teacher.

He touched his hat again. "Thank you, I'll give that careful consideration, Ma'am. The men who came by here won't bother you again, I promise you that."

He kicked his horse a little and rode off without sayin' anythin' more. I was havin' trouble followin' after him as Ef had quit pattin' my leg and had taken hold of it sort of high up like. I finally managed to kick my horse with my left leg and got my other leg free so's I could set off after Teacher who was the best part of a half mile off before I actually got goin'.

I caught up to him and we rode pretty quiet for a while. I was havin' some difficulty stayin' awake but the tracks was fresh enough that they was easy to follow when I bothered to look down. So far, a kid could've tracked those two. I hadn't actually been a whole lot of use to Teacher up to then, but he never said nothin' about it.

After we'd rode a ways Teacher looked over at me. "Looks to me like those women could use a man around the place. Big job for ladies, running a ranch."

I wasn't sure that particular coulee was one I wanted to ride into, so I kept quiet.

"Yes," he said. "Not that they aren't mighty capable ladies, especially that Ef. Fine woman, that one. Seems to me, a man could do worse than getting into the ranching business with two such fine women as that."

"I got a ranch," I said.

"Yes, you have," Teacher said, "but there are always things that can be done with ranches such as selling them, for instance."

I didn't say anything after that. Partly because I wasn't enjoyin' the conversation. Not that I hadn't already been thinkin' about what Teacher was sayin' even before he said it. Ef was a good woman and though she weren't no beauty, I've always believed a plough horse can be every bit as useful as a carriage horse and sometimes a damn sight more so, especially if the plough horse enjoyed evenin' activities as much as Ef appeared to. So, I'd been thinkin' about it all right, but I didn't feel like *talkin'* about it. The other reason I wasn't as interested in conversation as I might've been was that I kept fallin' asleep. In fact, I was asleep when I got shot.

At first, I didn't know I was shot. I was layin' there on the ground, more embarrassed than anythin' 'cause I figured I'd been sleepin' so hard I fell off my horse. But when I went to get up, I felt a big pain in my side and I looked down and there was blood, lots of it, all through my shirt and down onto my pants.

I looked up and Teacher said, "Are you okay?"

"Gutshot," I said, "but I don't think it's bad. Just caught me on the edge."

If I'd wanted to say more I'd've had to say it to myself because Teacher had his rifle out and was ridin like hell in the direction of a bluff of trees he must've figured the shot come from. I would've liked to help but my biggest problem was that when I moved sudden or took a deep breath, the pain in my side got right bold. If I just lay there quiet, it wasn't too bad. So, I lay there and watched Teacher get off a couple of shots at those trees. There was a bunch of dust along about that time and I figured whoever'd been shootin' at us had lit out.

The more I thought about it the more I didn't approve of Teacher ridin' right at 'em like that. If whoever it was that was hidin' there had been decent with a firearm or if there was a flock of renegade Indians there, he could've got himself killed right off. I didn't figure it was likely that whoever was doin' the shootin', if they'd've killed off Teacher, would've stopped there, if you see what I'm meanin'. So, I was awful glad when I saw that first cloud of dust headin' north in a real big hurry. I wasn't near as happy about the fact that a second cloud of dust, which was Teacher, was chasin' the first one and not showin' any signs of lettin' up. Pretty soon the dust disappeared altogether. I got to wonderin' if now that my job appeared to be done, Teacher expected me to make my own way home, belly wound and all.

He was gone about an hour, though it felt more like three. I was thinkin' about maybe tryin' to get over to my horse who was enjoyin' the grass a little ways off. That's when one of the dust clouds came back in sight. I was a little uneasy thinkin' about the fact Teacher could be coyote-food out on the prairie somewhere and whoever killed him was comin' for me.

That wasn't it though. When he was a mile or so off, I could see it was only one rider and it wasn't long till I could make out Teacher's sorrel horse.

"Get 'em?" I said as he came up and got off his horse.

"Nope." He shook his head. "Got close enough to scare them a little, but I figured I better get back here. "

"Sorry you had to come back."

"I should've come back quicker." Teacher started checkin' over my wound. "You're bleeding quite a bit."

"It ain't so bad," I said.

"Yeah."

He tore apart a shirt and stuffed some of it inside what was left of my shirt over where I was shot. Then he bandaged me up some.

"Hillier and Cox, was it?" I asked.

"That's right." He nodded. "I should've been paying closer attention. If I had've you wouldn't've got shot."

"I wasn't exactly alert myself at the time," I said.

"We're a couple of hours ride from Cut Bank." Teacher eased me up on my horse. "There'll be a doctor there. That's where we'll go."

"They'll get away from you," I told him as he mounted up on the paint.

"No, they won't," Teacher said. "You got me close enough. I can follow them from here."

"I'd like to go along with you," I said. "I don't feel like I've done much in the way of helpin' so far."

"We'll see what the doctor says about that."

The doctor didn't say much at first. That's because he was drunker than a billy goat once we found him, which took more time than the ride into town. Dennerty, he said his name was; the doctor was a young man and didn't seem to worry about much. Especially he didn't seem to worry about people in need of his services.

Once he was able to look me over, he said the bullet went right through, hadn't hit anythin' real important, and there was no reason I couldn't ride on once he sewed me up. I asked about the pain when I moved around and he said the bullet probably grazed a couple of my inside organs but that it didn't matter a hell of a lot, that's how he put it. I can't say I had a lot of confidence in Doc Dennerty at first, and his handlin' of the needle, what with the shakes he had, didn't make me feel a whole lot better. I'm pretty sure there's a few more puncture holes in my side than was absolutely necessary to get me patched, but I will admit that once he got done stitchin', along with the fact that he was willin' to share the whisky he carried around in a medicine bottle, I was pretty sure I could whip Hillier, Cox, Teacher and the entire James Gang if it come to that.

Teacher decided we wouldn't leave until the next morning, so I got to sleep under covers right there in Doc Dennerty's office. That was all right, I guess, but the bed was nothin' special. If I'd had my pick of preferences I'd've chose to be bedded down alongside them bushes with Ef. Although, truth is, she probably would've opened up my stitches and bled me to death what with the kind of carryin' on she appeared to favour.

When I woke up next mornin', the pain in my head was more severe by considerable than the one in my side, so Teacher figured we could ride out again.

"You aren't obliged to come if you don't care to," he told me. "You could be back at the Burnside ranch with the ladies by nightfall if you'd rather. I won't hold you to going with me."

Now until that moment I hadn't thought about the fact Ef and Hazel were a choice. I thought about it then but decided against goin' back. First of all, I felt I owed Teacher even if he said I didn't. I didn't feel right about leavin' with the job not done. Then too, there was the fact I didn't feel comfortable hobblin' back to Ef's ranch like a kicked dog after we'd set off like soldiers headin' for a battle. I wasn't sure Ef would take to a man who admitted he was licked before the fight even started.

"I'd prefer to ride with you," I said to Teacher.

We mounted up and rode out of Cut Bank a couple of hours later. If I'd known what was to come, I would've chosen otherwise — limpin' back to the ladies ranch or even settin' around getting' drunk with Doc Dennerty would've beat the hell out of what was to happen once we was clear of Cut Bank.

Chapter Eleven

We didn't travel fast. I guess that was partly so's not to do any more damage to the hole in my side, and partly because Teacher knew we'd be able to find Cox and Hillier no matter how far, or how fast, they travelled. We rode northwest out of Cutbank and hadn't gone five miles when we come to a small ranch sittin' on the flat prairie like a pimple on a chin. As we approached it, the first person I saw was a woman. She was behind a horse and the two of them was pullin' a stump out of the ground. I looked at that woman for a while and then I turned to Teacher.

"If this is another ladies' ranch and if we get asked to sleep in the barn again, I'll be ridin' back to town," I told him. "I figured I should tell you that right off so's there's no confusion."

I guess as much as I enjoyed that night with Ef, it scared me some, too. My experience with women before her was what you'd call limited and if they was all like Ef, I figured I'd better be a bit sparin' in my partnerin' up. Especially gutshot, as I was.

Teacher, he just grinned. Right after that we saw a man out back of the house with an axe and I felt a lot less stormy in the guts. It didn't turn out to matter much as we wasn't stoppin' anyway but to water the horses. We chatted with the man and his wife while the horses drank. The woman looked like she'd be havin a little one pretty soon and I figured gee hawin' that horse around like she was must've been mighty hard.

Then we touched our hats, wished them good luck and rode off. Teacher asked me if my side could take a little faster pace and I told him I'd prefer lopin' to trottin'. For the next couple of hours, we covered a good piece of ground.

As we travelled, I noticed a good-sized cloud formin' in the sky up ahead of us. The bigger the cloud got, the blacker it got, and it soon became clear that it had a mind to storm.

"I hear these Canadian storms can be pretty bad," I said. I had to talk louder than usual because the wind was gettin' up.

"Could be," Teacher said, "but I don't know that we're in Canada yet."

That was the last piece of conversation we was to have for a long time. We got our slickers on and tied our hats onto our heads. We no sooner had that done than the very worst storm I ever saw hit. There was plenty of rain, and some snow, and it was comin' right into our faces. It was all I could do to keep my horse movin' forward. He kept wantin' to turn his back end into the storm and I would've let him except that I was pretty sure Teacher was probably pluggin' on straight ahead. That was a bit of a guess on my part because about five minutes after the storm hit us full out, I lost Teacher. I tried callin' a few times but that was a waste of breath. The words just got blowed back into my mouth.

Then I tried zig-zaggin back and forth for a while thinkin' I might stumble across him eventually. But I didn't. It came down so hard that for a long time I couldn't see my horse's head. I reached down and shook his mane every once in a while just to make sure he was there. He could've drowned and slid right out from under me and I wouldn't't've known about it except my legs would've been stuck knee deep in mud. I might've figured it out then.

That horse of mine, his name was Rascal, he'd seen plenty of storms too, but nothin' like this one that I was pretty sure had come down from Canada. Except that I heard the ones from up there all had more snow in 'em than this one did. Anyway, Rascal stayed under me and on his feet, which was about the only good thing about that whole day.

We kept movin', the two of us, the rest of the day and most of the night. I wasn't sure where we were but unless the storm had shifted, I figured we was still makin' our way north, although we weren't all that quick about it. Now I should explain that in my whole life up to about three days previous, the most excitin' thing that had happened to me was when I shot Joe Metzger's dog 'cause we thought he had the rabies. Turns out he didn't but it was a mistake anybody could've made. Joe Metzger didn't see it that way though and we ain't been close ever since. Sure, I've tracked critters and men, some bad ones in both groups, but I never was the one to be involved in the dispute settlin' once my trackin' was done. Also, I ain't been a drinkin' man, nor one to go off with sportin' women, and I ride safe horses and stay out of fights. Now, here it was, in the space of three days and nights, I'd done things I didn't even know the name for with a woman I'd had the acquaintance of for maybe four hours, I'd got drunk on a doctor's whisky, I'd got myself shot by somebody I'd never seen, and if all that weren't enough, I was lost in a storm that might've been one of them Canadian ones. Even if it wasn't, I didn't know where I was, Montana or Canada, and me and my horse were so wet I figured both of us could drown from the inside out. I was beginnin' to think a whole week with Teacher would be more excitement than a farm boy like me could stand.

I didn't know how long I'd been ridin'. The storm hadn't let up any, maybe was worse, if anything, and I was awful hungry which was a bad thing since Teacher was carryin' what food we had. Then Rascal up and stopped. Stopped cold. Wouldn't take another step. I kicked him, smacked his back end and called him some of the names I'd picked up in conversation with Ef, but nothin' worked. So, I got down out of the saddle, went around to the front of him to see if I could lead him and walked smack into a fair-sized tree sittin' in the middle of some scrub brush. That horse figured out that if we hunkered down on the downwind side of that wide tree trunk, our situation would be improved. I surveyed things and had to agree with him. I got him turned and backed him up against that tree trunk. Then I got crouched down right between his front legs. We wasn't exactly comfortable, understand, but it was a whole lot better than ridin' along into a storm that was never goin to quit, not ever.

Next thing that happened was I woke up. Now there's some that may not believe this, but I ended up layin' under my horse with his legs set around me like four posts, the ones you see on them fancy beds. If that horse had moved any one of his feet, he'd've had to end up standin' on me. Mind, I probably would've just made a squishin' noise if he had stepped on me. But he didn't, that's the thing. Stood statue still for I have no idea how long in that storm and wind, and you know how crazy horses can get in wind, until I woke up.

The strangest thing of all was there was another tree a little ways off about the same size as the one Rascal and me was under. And under that tree was the biggest old coyote you ever saw. He was mindin' his own business and just tryin' to stay dry. He didn't seem to care one damn about Rascal and me. It was like him and Rascal made a deal between 'em and I didn't matter. Eventually, the coyote trotted off without so much as a look back.

The storm had pretty well quit but it was still cloudy, and the wind was still blowin' out of the north. It was too cold to dry out and I had this feelin', one I'd never had before in my life. I would've given up my share of the ranch for a hot bath and a warm, dry bed. That wasn't likely to happen out there on the prairie, so I figured my best bet was to keep goin' north till I got to the Milk River. My guess was that Teacher would do the same thing and maybe we'd meet up.

I got Rascal movin' — he wasn't crazy about the idea — and we got to the river a few hours later. I knew that if I didn't find Teacher soon, I'd have to shoot somethin' to eat. The sun had come out and it was considerable warmer, so I decided to let Rascal graze a spell while I dried out. Even with my slicker over top of me, every single piece of clothing I had on was wetter 'n a fish's belly so I decided to peel everythin' off and set it on rocks to unwet itself. Then I laid out on the grass next to the clothes to do the same. I managed to get a little sleep. When I woke up, Teacher was sittin' on his horse lookin' at me, not mad like, but not real happy either. I don't know how long he'd been sittin' there.

"See you haven't drowned or bled to death yet," he said.

"I was plannin' to go lookin' for you right after I rested up." I sat up kind of quick. I was feelin' a little uncomfortable with my clothes spread all over the place and none of 'em on me.

"Guess you won't have to now," Teacher said.

"One good thing about that there storm," I said. "I expect Hillier and Cox was caught up in it same as us. They'll be easy to follow in the mud."

"We'll probably find them naked and sleeping somewhere down river." He smiled at me then and that's how I knew he wasn't mad or anythin'.

All the same, I had a feelin' that last remark was meant to get me movin' so I stood up and started gatherin' up things to wear. Some of 'em at least was getting' close to bein' dry. I pulled my trousers on first since I was still kind of embarrassed about bein' found buck naked on the prairie. While I was getting' gathered up, Teacher handed me a piece of jerky and a hunk of cheese and I ate that down kinda quick as I was buttonin' my shirt.

"Getting shot doesn't seem to have affected your appetite," he said.

"It's been a spell between meals," I said.

"True," he nodded at my side, "how's the wound?"

"Tell the truth, I ain't looked at it for a while," I told him, "but it feels pretty good."

"Tonight, we'll change that bandage and I'll mix up a little something to put on there," he said.

I was ready to go, so I mounted up and asked him what the plan was. "Sure hope we ain't thinkin' about crossin' that river," I said as we got a little closer to it.

Ef had told us it was high and that was before the storm which I figured must've raised it up a bunch. There'd be no way to cross but to swim the horses over and Rascal, he's a capable enough swimmer but not fond of it. Whenever we'd approached water in the past, he had generally spilled me off on the ground three or four times before I was able to convince him to go to swimmin'. I figured this time would be no different.

"We might not have to," Teacher said. "The storm might have kept them on this side of the river. We'll ride west for a while, see if we can pick up their trail."

We rode back from the river a half mile or better. Teacher figured all the brush growin' along the river banks would make good cover if Cox and Hillier decided to ambush us again. I figured even an ambush was preferable to havin' to swim Rascal across the Milk.

We rode fifteen or twenty miles and didn't see any sign of the men we were chasin'. I concluded that maybe Hillier and Cox got this far before the storm hit and maybe even crossed the river. Teacher must've been thinkin' along the same lines 'cause we rode another few miles or so and then stopped.

"We're crossing," he said.

I nodded but I didn't say anythin' since I didn't want him to know I was a little anxious about river crossin's and that Rascal was a lot more anxious about 'em than me. We rode back to the bank of the river and it didn't look too bad, although as soon as we came nose to nose with the water itself, Rascal started prancin' which I well knew was just the preliminaries to what would happen if I pressed the matter. We'd been hearin' a growin' roar for some time as we'd been ridin'. I figured it was probably rapids and a bit of white water but that wasn't it at all. As we looked downstream, we could see that the river took a bit of a bend and right there was a falls. It wasn't a big falls, I couldn't tell if maybe it was just somethin' caused by the high water or what, but it was a falls all right. The thing is, right above the falls the riverbed widened out some and got shallow enough that we'd be able to walk across.

Teacher pointed — it was getting' pretty loud for regular talkin' what with the roar from them falls, and we rode down a piece. The horses didn't like the noise much and acted like they was spooked, but we got there and got 'em into the river. The riverbed was, I don't know, a couple of decent rock throws across and we was about halfway over when all hell broke loose.

We was bein' shot at again. The worst of it was there wasn't a whole lot in the middle of that river for cover. The shots were comin' from the north side so we couldn't go that way and it looked awful unlikely that we'd get back to the south side without gettin' killed first. I guess that's why Teacher did what he did. I never did ask him about it, but I've thought a lot about it since.

All of a sudden, he yelled, "Come on," and he started overin' and underin' his horse and racin' straight at the falls. Now I'm not an educated man but I don't think of myself as completely foolish either and I don't think that would've been my choice if I'd been leadin' the expedition. But since I wasn't, and bein' as how I had some strong worries about what would happen if I stayed where I was, I lit out after him, just prayin' every step that Rascal wouldn't go down. Runnin' over wet rocks at top speed on shod horses is what most folks would call an unsettlin' way to travel, but then bullets can be a mite unsettlin' theirselves. I was thinkin' Teacher would veer off at the last second and we'd try to get behind some rocks or somethin' and shoot it out with whoever had ambushed us which I expected was probably the two men we was followin'.

But that wasn't his plan. I discovered what his plan was about three seconds before it stopped bein' a plan and started bein' a situation. He never once stopped spurrin' and whippin' that horse and the next thing I knew he disappeared. Rode plumb over the falls. Worst part was, even if Rascal and me had wanted to stop, we couldn't't've got it done in time on those rocks and in that water. Plus, I ain't at all sure Rascal wanted to stop.

On the way down I remember thinkin' the whole time. It wasn't a long falls, but when you and your horse have just gone over it, even if it's only twenty or thirty feet, it feels like a couple of miles so a person can get quite an amount of thinkin' done. What I was thinkin' about was boulders. The ones I figured we'd land on when we got to the bottom of the falls and which would kill us all deader'n mud. Rascal and me parted company about halfway down.

What happened next isn't all that clear to me even now and I've done a pile of recollectin' on the matter. I remember a lot of foam down there which meant I wouldn't't've seen the boulders if there had been any. But there wasn't, at least not where I landed, nor Rascal neither because one of the first things I do recall is Rascal goin' by me real fast. Suddenly he was a swimmin' fool. I grabbed a rein as he was racin' by and hung on like hell. He fought hard because I'd pulled his head around when I grabbed that rein and I think he was worryin' about drownin'. So was I, which is why I grabbed the rein in the first place. And much as I liked my horse, he was probably as good as I'd ever had, if I had to choose which of us was goin' to drown, he would've been my unanimous pick.

I tried to help him by swimmin' a little myself but what with me in my boots and clothes and him in his saddle and all, I figured both of us was makin' our last swim. That's when out of the blue, Rascal got his feet on the bottom. I hadn't let go of that rein and I managed to pull myself into the saddle and we headed for shore — the south shore.

Of course, as soon as I got there, I looked around for Teacher, but I didn't see him right off. Now I know it ain't right to speak disrespectful of them that's gone, but right about that time, I can't say the thoughts I was havin' about my travelin' partner were all that flatterin'. So far, durin' the time he was in command, we'd encountered questionable women and surgeons, got ourselves ambushed twice and rode over a waterfall. And, so far, the only casualty of the war was me. Our enemies didn't seem to be sufferin' a whole lot. And now, here I was at the bottom of that falls, not sure if Teacher was alive or dead, but even if he was alive, I was plumb positive that if Hillier and Cox came ridin' along — *beside* the falls like sane men, not over them — they'd kill us quicker than a snakebite because every piece of armament we was carryin' (Teacher was carryin' several) would be too wet to be of any use for some time.

I rode in behind some bushes for cover. Rascal kept shakin' himself and I kept tryin' to get him to stop. A shakin' horse and a spray of water from behind a bunch of bushes will tell even a stupid tracker that somebody might be hidin' in there. I stayed behind them bushes for quite a while but for reasons I'll never figure out the ambushers never came down to finish us off. Maybe they figured we'd taken care of that for them with the jump over the falls. Come to think of it, that would've been a reasonable conclusion on their part.

I'd been tucked away in that brush for maybe a half hour and I decided I'd best try to make a move. I rode out from behind my cover and who's the first person I saw but Teacher. Only thing was he was on the other side of the river.

He waved at me, one of those 'come on over' waves. I wasn't sure how to tell Rascal we was goin' to have to go back into the water. That horse, by that time must've been confused as to whether he was horse or pickerel. Sure enough, and I can't honestly say I blame him, when I aimed him at the river, he ducked his head and went to buckin'. What saved me, I guess, was the fact that the saddle, bein' waterlogged as it was, must've weighed out like a yearling steer. That, and with him bein' tired from all that swimmin', Rascal couldn't get a whole lot of power into his jumpin' and kickin' and I was able to ride him out of it. I swear as we rode into that water again, I felt that horse sigh, exactly the way folks do when there's no way around doin' somethin they hate, like pickin' rocks.

Anyway, we swum over and come up on the other bank and rode up to Teacher. He didn't say anythin' but handed me my hat which he must've fished out of the river during all the excitement. I hadn't even noticed it was gone.

We rode a ways off from the falls so's we could hear each other. When we stopped, Teacher said, "You still all right, healthwise?"

"Yeah," I said, "but I doubt I'll ever be thirsty again."

He nodded and smiled.

"Why do those fellas keep ambushin' us?" I wondered. "Seems like every time they do that, they let us get closer to 'em."

"I guess they think that's their best hope," Teacher said. "They probably realize, with a tracker like you and gun handler like me, we'll eventually get them if they don't get us first." He kind of laughed when he said that like maybe he realized our trackin' and gun handlin' hadn't been all that impressive so far. Although if you ask me, there wasn't a lot wrong with the trackin' part of our mission.

Anyhow, I didn't find that particular piece of information all that comfortin'. "So, there could be another ambush comin' just about any old time."

"We'll be ready for them next time," Teacher said. "Though I doubt there'll be one. They likely think we're either dead or we live charmed lives. Either way they'll be riding on. The pace of their journey will tell us which of the two ways of thinking they're favouring."

"I'm awful wet again," I said.

"I'm a little damp myself." Teacher nodded. "We'll eat and rest while our clothes dry out and then we'll be moving as fast as you can stand to go."

I told him I figured I'd be able to move along at a pretty reasonable speed once we was dry. We stripped down — not quite naked this time — laid out our saddles and the rest of our gear alongside our clothes and let the horses graze while we had another meal of cheese and jerky. It wasn't that either of us was real fond of that combination, but most of the food we had was ruined by the amount of water it had taken on. The cheese and jerky for that matter wasn't exactly improved by them bein' drug through most of the territory's large bodies of water.

As we were eatin', I decided to ask Teacher something I'd been ponderin' on since we'd been out there chasin' bandits.

"Why are you after Hillier and Cox anyway?"

"They tried to shoot me. Three times now, as a matter of fact."

"Yeah, but if you hadn't gone after 'em after that first time, chances are they would've just rode off and let things be," I said.

Teacher worked some jerky around in his mouth. "That's probably so," he said, "but I've concluded over the years that the best policy is not to let people get away with shooting at you. Even if they run like hell afterwards. Gets other people to thinking maybe they can get away with the same sort of thing. That can lead to dangerous situations."

I could see the logic in that, and I told him so. He surprised me then by tellin' me somethin' I hadn't expected to hear.

"Besides it'll be two less I have to shoot later."

I don't even think I got out a response when he said that. I just looked at him.

"There's someone needs killing back in Kecking Horse. I'm not sure who that person is, though I have an idea. If I'm right, then he's been lining up guns for the day our showdown comes. I'm just eliminating a couple of those guns."

I thought about that. About the only person I'd heard had been doin' any hirin' lately was Mr. J. Emerson Keymore.

"You mean Mr. Keymore?"

"We'll see." Teacher handed me another piece of jerky.

Teacher fixed up a roots and mud concoction he said he'd learned from a Sioux woman in Wyoming and he slapped that on my wound with a clean bandage. We rode out a little while later in clothes that were as close to dry as they'd been in quite some time. I thought about how doin' what we'd been doin' the last while had ruled out the need for clothes launderin'. If a fella was lookin' for a positive, that was about it.

Teacher had said we'd be movin' fast and fast was how we moved. The trackin' was easy—hooves leave marked impressions in mud — and we could tell that Hillier and Cox were also travelin' in a hurry. Accordin' to Teacher's theory that was because they thought we were charmed men and were scared of us. I was hopin' they were right.

There was one more distraction that slowed us up before we got down to the business of metin' out punishment. Now you may come away with a feelin' that what I'm goin' to tell you doesn't have a whole lot to do with anythin'. And maybe it doesn't but I wanted to get it down here so's I could remember it pretty clear thirty or forty years from now when I might want to tell my grandchildren about it. Though I might not since I wouldn't want to be scarin' 'em.

We were well into Canada for sure by then, a little south of a place called Fort Macleod. Like I was tellin' you, we was travelin' as fast as the horses could stand. Teacher's horse threw a front shoe and it looked like we might be slowed up. But it turned out better than it could've since we could see a homestead not far off and headed straight for it.

We got there in a half hour or so. The place was populated by a number of people. One of 'em was a man with the biggest moustache I'd ever seen in my life. He was Cain. I never figured out if Cain was his first name or his last. He never said. He had a very pretty wife, a small woman, he said her name was Annie, and there was kids everywhere like when you pull an old board off the barn floor and mice scatter every which way. Since Teacher and me, neither one of us knew where Cain fit in in terms of names, we couldn't call the woman Mrs. Cain and, of course, we weren't about to call her Annie, so we just referred to her as Ma'am, part out of respect and part out of necessity.

The place was run down pretty bad. The main reason for that, we found out, was that the one thing Cain didn't do around that farm was work. When he saw that Teacher's sorrel needed a shoe, he said, "Annie. She'll fix you up. She know's where everything is."

He pointed and his wife headed off toward a building that looked half barn and half shed. Teacher followed after her and I started that way myself. Cain stopped me.

"Fish," he said.

"What?"

"Fish. You fish?"

"Well ... uh ... yeah."

"Good." He strode off in a way that told me I was supposed to go along.

We walked up a little rise in back of his place. When we got to the top of the rise, I noticed a pond with a stream leadin' into it. At the edge of the pond was a boat, a rowboat. Now the thing was, the pond was maybe twenty feet across in both directions. Two pulls on the oars and you'd be stuck hard to the other bank. But, he got in the boat and pointed like he wanted me to get in too. There were a couple of fishin poles in the bottom of the boat.

"Well ... I don't know," I said. "I don't expect Teacher will be long and ..."

"Trout," Cain said.

It appeared to me that this was a man who believed one word was all a sentence needed. Bit like his name, I suppose.

Now I like trout and I figured Teacher'd be fifteen minutes anyways puttin' that shoe back on. I got to thinkin' about what a fine meal trout would make that night after all the cheese and jerky we'd been consumin' of late. So, I got in the boat and we pushed off into the middle of that pond. And there we sat, lookin' strange, if you ask me, in that we could've fished off the shore just as easy. Yet there we was, two grown men in a boat fishin' for trout in a piece of water not much bigger than a bathtub.

Cain caught hisself a trout right off and I got a nice one a few minutes later. I got to wishin' we could make a day of catchin' fish in that little pond with trees on three sides and water gurglin' into it from a stream to the east.

"Ghosts," Cain said, and he set his pole down.

"What?"

"Ghosts. Just north of here. Mile or so. Kids. Diphtheria. Three of 'em. All died the same week. Some days you hear 'em playin on them rope swings near the house. Heard 'em yesterday."

I was havin' a little trouble followin' the path of the conversation. Partly because Cain had a peculiar way of expressin' what was on his mind and partly because another fish was on my hook and my attention was somewhat headed off in that direction.

"Three kids died?" I said.

"Yep. In 93. Diphtheria got 'em. Nobody there now. But you hear 'em some days. Laughin' and playin' in the yard."

I landed the trout, all the while wonderin' why Cain had decided I needed to know about them diptheria kids. I suppose I always believed in ghosts all right, though I'd never had no ghost experience as such. Funny thing was, that little pond that had been about the peacefullest place in the world a few minutes before, started to feel dark and, well, I admit it, scary. So, I was about half glad when I heard Teacher yell that we was goin'.

Cain gave a pull on the oars and we were ashore. I gathered up my fish, thanked him for a pleasant afternoon and skedaddled back to the house. I was mounted up ready to go before Teacher was even saddled.

"You're in a hurry all of a sudden." He looked at me.

"Me? No, I ain't. Just thought you might be is all."

Cain's wife smiled at me. Then she come closer and whispered up at me, "He been tellin' them ghosty stories to ya? He does that every time we get visitors. Don't worry, though. Them kids'll not bother ya."

I noticed she hadn't said there ain't no such kids, just that they wouldn't bother us. It looked to me like that woman was a believer herself in them ghost children.

She handed me a piece of old newsprint to wrap our fish in, and Teacher and me, we touched our hats and rode out of there. That was probably as glad as I've ever been to be leavin' a place, even though Cain and the lady and the kids all seemed friendly enough.

We headed north toward Fort Macleod. As soon as we were out of sight of the house, I looked over at Teacher.

"Might be a good idea to veer off a little bit."

"Oh?" he said. "Why's that?"

"Oh ... uh, Cain ... he told me there's trouble up here a ways. Uh ... quicksand, I think he said."

"Really."

"Yeah." I nodded hard. "We might be wise to swing west a spell, then come back to this line after we've gone a few miles."

"Well." Teacher rubbed his hand up and down his jaw. "I've never seen quicksand before. And especially I haven't seen any on the dry plains. So maybe we should keep riding right the way we are and have a look."

"I don't know if that's a good idea," I said.

"And anyway, I'd kind of like to see if those ghost kids are out there playing on the swing today."

"Oh," I said. I knew that while he was fixin' that shoe, Cain's wife must've been talkin' to him about the exact same thing Cain was talkin' to me about up there in the boat.

There was no point arguin' about it, so I just rode along.

I swear I heard the sound before I even saw the swings. Kids laughin', yellin' and it sounded like water splashin' like they had a tub of water and was flingin' it around like kids will on a hot day. I was sure we was about to come onto another farm real similar to the one we'd just left.

In fact, I said as much to Teacher, but he didn't answer. We come up over a little rise and that's when I saw it. It was a farm, all right, but there wasn't any farmin' bein' done there, hadn't been for some time. The house was fallin' down pretty bad although the barn looked in fair shape. Of course, out here, homesteaders had always put a lot more stock in their barns than they did in their houses on account of you wouldn't last long if your animals weren't looked after. So that explained why the barn and corrals were standin' up a whole lot better than the house and yard. The yard was pretty much overrun with weeds and brush but here and there a flower still gave a bit of colour to the place.

The swings was hangin' from a thick branch of a cottonwood, a little south and east of the house. But there was no water and no tub. And no kids. Not at first. But I swear to you I had heard 'em as sure as I'm writin' this down. Once we come over the rise, the noise of the kids stopped, just like it might've if they'd seen strangers ride in when they was alive. And as we rode by, I was as sure as I've been of anythin' in my life that I saw a kid, a little gal with yellow hair, lots of it, peekin' around the corner of the barn. I was of a mind to go back and ask Cain what them ghost kids looked like. But I didn't. And when I looked again, the yellow-haired little gal was gone, and the yard was as still as I've ever seen a place.

Except for one thing. A couple of them swings was movin' back and forth like they was bein' moved by the wind. 'Cept there was no wind, not a breath of 'er.

We never stopped and when I asked Teacher if he'd heard 'em or seen that little gal he didn't answer me, just looked at me with a little smile that was on his mouth but not in his eyes. And I noticed he removed his hat while we rode by that place. I did the same.

The actual killin' of Hillier and Cox didn't amount to that much after all the excitement of just catchin 'em. We rode into the town of Fort Macleod and stopped at the fort there. Teacher talked to a couple of army fellas and we rode right off headin' north.

"They're trying to make a place maybe sixty, seventy miles north of here called The Crossing, on the Highwood River." Teacher said. "But the sergeant said they weren't going all that fast anymore. We should catch them well before that."

He was right. For the first time in all our dealin's with Hillier and Cox, we saw them before they saw us. They was camped by a place called Mosquito Creek Crossing. Turns out

Hillier'd eaten somethin' in Fort Macleod and had a bad case of the diarrhea. Ridin' horseback ain't no treat when you got the runs so I couldn't blame them for stoppin'.

They didn't appear to be expectin' us at all. We left the horses and walked the last few hundred yards on foot. We looked in on them from behind some tree cover. One of them was bent over with his britches down around his ankles. Teacher whispered to me that was Hillier. Cox was laid out on a blanket. He looked like he was sleepin', though there was still a couple of hours of daylight left.

I figured Teacher would wait until Hillier finished up and at least had his trousers back in place. But he didn't. Motioned to me to stay behind the trees and then he stood up and walked in there with that .44 in his hand.

"Afternoon boys," he said. "You never should've shot at me. Not the first time, nor the second nor the third."

Then he shot Hillier who'd made the mistake of tryin' to reach for a rifle that was propped up against a log right next to where he was ... well, you know.

Cox jumped up and looked around like he wasn't sure where he was. He had a gun on his hip but had the good sense to leave it there for the moment. Teacher was talkin' real quiet so I couldn't hear what he was saying. But he was talkin' and walkin' toward Cox at the same time. I could see Cox shaking his head and motionin' with his hands like he was wantin' Teacher to go away and leave him alone.

Eventually he went for that gun on his hip. Desperate thinkin', I guess. Maybe he figured Teacher would kill him anyway. Or maybe that's what Teacher was tellin' him. I don't know which it was to this day.

Of course, when his hand went to his hip, Teacher shot him. Gut shot. A lot worse than mine because his was smack in the middle, where mine was just a twitch in the side. Cox fell on his back and went to makin' awful noises. Sort of like a cow bellerin' when her calf won't come. It must've been real awful for him because he didn't die right away. Which lookin' back on it, is how I figure Teacher had it planned.

I stayed back and Teacher walked up and kneeled down alongside Cox who was still bellerin'. I could see them talkin'. Cox kept shakin' his head, but finally he stopped and said some things I couldn't hear. After a while the bellerin' dropped down to more like a whimper and then he stopped movin' or makin' any noise at all. I figure that's when he died. Teacher stood up and holstered his gun and started walkin' back toward me. I stepped out from behind the trees.

"Want me to get started buryin' 'em?" I said.

"No," he shook his head. "They can stay where they are. The coyotes and crows can have them. We're leaving."

I didn't feel good about leavin' those men there even though I knew they'd've done the same thing if they'd gunned us first. But I also knew there was no point in debatin' the topic with Teacher.

"What was you talkin' about with that man while he was dyin'?" I asked him.

"He told me what I wanted to know."

That's all he said and then we mounted up and rode back to Kecking Horse without another incident worth the tellin'. Except that we stopped at Fort Macleod on the way back so Teacher could pay his respects at the grave of a scout named Jerry Potts who'd died a few months earlier. Potts scouted with my father years before but I didn't know him. I was in somethin' of a hurry to get home, but Teacher said we had to stop at that grave. So, we did.

Oh, and we cooked up them trout later that night. They was special after days of dried meat and cheese.

(That ends Cal Chapin's part of the story. To tell the truth, I was a little disappointed with the way he decided to end it off, just stopping all of a sudden like that. But that's the way Cal is, if you know him. Still I hope I'll be able to write a better finish to my part of this.)

Chapter Twelve

After what you just read, my guess is you'd be thinking all Hell was about to break loose when Teacher got back to Kecking Horse. He'd just killed off two of Mr. J. Emerson Keymore's hired men. And according to Cal Chapin, Teacher had his suspicions, whatever they were, pretty much confirmed during his talk with Cox as he was dying.

But when he got back, Teacher didn't do anything. Not a thing. He was idler than Cooper Raine in summer heat. Didn't go back to teaching. Didn't shoot anybody. He was just there. I'd see him around town a lot. He'd come into the store often and we'd talk some, but he wouldn't stay long. I noticed he didn't joke or smile as much as he used to.

He went back to staying out by the new school at night, even though he didn't have anything to do with it anymore. I didn't go out there to visit him. He didn't invite me, and I didn't feel right about stopping by uninvited. Mind you, I did occasionally get out to the school during the day. That's because I rode out there at the end of classes a couple of times to visit Miss Lyla Case. I guess you might say that after that night of the dance when I won the bet and danced with Sarah-Beth and the other ladies, I got some confidence in myself as far as with women and such.

On one of those occasions that I visited with Miss Lyla Case at the school and rode back to town with her — that was my excuse for going out there in the first place — I asked her if she'd like to go for a buggy ride and picnic the following Sunday after church. She accepted the invitation. If she hadn't done that and if we hadn't been out buggy riding that day, I guess this account of what happened never would have come to pass seeing as I wouldn't have been there.

Sunday came along and after church was out of the way, I went and got Mr. Westover's buckboard and Miss Lyla Case and I headed out south into the Indian Head Valley. It seemed like winter had forgotten us and the weather was almost spring-like. We'd been jogging along for a couple of hours and talking like we were brother and sister. We talked about a lot of things, but we spent quite a bit of time discussing horses. Miss Lyla Case, it turned out was very interested in horses, mostly because she hadn't been around them much. She asked me about breaking them and I yammered on like Virgil Watts on the subject of breaking and training horses.

Then I asked her if she'd like to take the reins for a while and she said she would. The horse was a quiet old thing, so Miss Lyla Case was pretty soon taking us down that road like an experienced teamster. I figured with her driving and me sitting there with nothing to do, it was the perfect opportunity to read a poem I'd copied out of a book with the idea of reading it to her at just such an appropriate moment.

It was a love poem from the sixteenth century. A guy named Edmund Spenser wrote it and I figured he must really have been in love with the lady in the poem because he wrote more than one hundred poems for her altogether. I'll put it down here so that you'll know what it was I was reading to Miss Lyla Case that afternoon.

Happy ye leaves, when as those lilly hands,
Which hold my life in their dead doing might,
Shall handle you and hold in loves soft bands,
Like captives trembling at the victors sight.
And happy lines, on which with starry light,
Those lamping eyes will deign sometimes to look,
And read the sorrows of my dying spright,
Written with tears in harts close bleeding book.
And happy rhymes, bathed in the sacred brook,
Of Helicon where she derived is,
When ye behold that Angels blessed look,
My soul's long lacked food, my heavens bliss,
Leaves, lines, and rhymes, seek her to please alone,

Whom if ye please, I care for other none.

I read it to her, and it was a long time before she said anything.

"It's a beautiful poem," is what she finally said.

"Yes'm, it is that," I said.

"Were you intending that the poem should express your feelings for me?" She looked over at me.

Well, I figured the combination of my new woman-confidence since the dance and the sentiments of Edmund Spenser was pretty much overpowering, so I looked right back at her.

"Yes, Miss Lyla Case, that is what I was intending."

"I see," she said.

As soon as she said, 'I see,' I knew Miss Lyla Case was, for good and all, not interested in being any more than brother and sister close, you remember I mentioned that earlier. I'd suspected it before, of course, but that moment pretty much convinced me that my first inclination had been correct.

"What about you and Sarah-Beth?" she asked me. "I thought you two were ..."

She never got the chance to finish that thought and I never got the chance to answer because a bullet whistled over us and dug itself into a mound of dirt to our left. Now I did say that the horse was quiet, but he wasn't so quiet that he took pleasure in being shot at. The next thing I knew we were racing down the road as fast as that old gelding's legs could make it happen. Somehow Miss Lyla Case got the reins back into my hands and her arms around my waist, tighter than a four-strand wire fence, and we covered ground; her, I think, hoping the experience would end soon and me kind of wishing it might last a few hours, more or less to establish the mood I wanted for the picnic. I don't really think she was hanging on because she was scared. I think it was more so she wouldn't get thrown out of the buckboard. But I liked it all the same. I guess I was still thinking that with some luck and a few more poems, I could overcome her romantic reluctance as it related to me. Of course, there was the matter of the bullet but just at that moment, it was secondary in my mind to having Miss Lyla Case attached to me like a sucker to stream scum.

My attention got diverted then due to the fact that there were more shots. We could hear them up ahead maybe a mile or so and beyond some low hills off to our right a ways. I got the old gelding slowed down, probably because he realized if he kept running that hard, he'd end up dead in a heap right there on that road before we went much further.

"Stray bullet," I told Miss Lyla Case. "I doubt if it was intended for us. Probably hunters."

That's what I said to her, but, of course, I was thinking hard about how this was the same territory where both Virgil Watts and I were jumped. The good thing was, I didn't totally succeed in quieting Miss Lyla Case's nerves and she was still wrapped around me and sitting so close I could almost feel her face against mine.

Actually, what we'd ridden into was both gunfight *and* ambush, but it was a little while before we found that out.

"Maybe we better take a look," I said and even though Miss Lyla Case was a mite nervous, she didn't say no to the idea.

We drove off the road into a field of prairie wool to our right. We came up over a rise and what we saw untangled Miss Lyla Case's arms from me in a hurry. I have to admit I was forced to focus my thoughts, and other energies in another direction, that being straight ahead.

"They're shooting at the school!" Miss Lyla Case yelled in a voice I'd never heard from her before.

She was right. A bunch of riders were spread out over a few hundred yards maybe a half mile from the new schoolhouse and they were filling it full of gunfire. We watched for a minute or two, I suppose more stunned than anything else at what we were seeing. I'll have to be honest and tell you that at first, I couldn't understand why men would want to spend a Sunday afternoon firing into an empty building.

It was a couple of minutes of non-stop gunfire before I realized the schoolhouse wasn't empty. What drew that to my attention was a number of puffs of smoke at a couple of windows of the school. That, and the fact the men who were shooting *at* the school seemed to be getting more and more uncomfortable as a result of whoever it was that was shooting *from* the school.

"We've got to stop them," Miss Lyla Case said in a way that left no doubt that she meant it. "What should we do?"

She turned to me as she asked the question. I looked as sage as it's possible for someone with a nose like mine to look and shaded my eyes with one hand as I regarded the situation.

"We'd best go for help," I said, although the way I said it, you might have thought I was asking as opposed to answering.

"No," said Miss Lyla Case, "that's not it."

I shook my head vigorously to indicate I agreed that that was not it.

"Whoever's in the school could be dead by the time we got back," she said.

And with that declaration having been made, Miss Lyla Case grabbed the reins — you will recall that she had only moments before completed her first driving lesson — and whipped the gelding into a high lope. Both the gelding and I were taken very much by surprise by this turn of events, me to the point that I sat silent as we raced across the prairie straight at the school.

Apparently, the horse and I were not alone in our reaction to Miss Lyla Case's course of action. As we ran straight at the left flank of the attackers, the two southernmost riders backed their horses up to let us through and the rest of the shooters' guns fell silent. Miss Lyla Case, however, was not silent. She was "Yah"ing as loud as any teamster had ever "Yah"ed.

While we were moving quite fast, there's no doubt we could have got to the school quicker if we'd travelled in a straight line. That was the one thing we were definitely not doing. Now I have never sailed the high seas, in fact, I've never even seen a sea, high or otherwise, but I know people who have been on large sailing ships and they have referred to something called tacking. As I understand it, tacking is a method of getting somewhere straight ahead by steering first to the left and then to the right of the place you're trying to go. This is so you can gain maximum benefit from the wind is how these friends of mine have explained it. Though there was no hint of a breeze blowing that Sunday afternoon, Miss Lyla Case and I were tacking our way toward the school.

Of course, we didn't know who was inside shooting back at the men on the outside. It was certainly possible it was Teacher who was in there, but it was just as possible that it wasn't. And with the buggy zig-zagging back and forth over a chunk of prairie that was plumb full of gopher and badger holes, I hadn't had much opportunity to get a look at the people who were pumping lead into the school. Or at least had been. They weren't shooting now, and it occurred to me the reason for the break in the gunfire might have been that watching our buggy ride might have been more entertaining than shooting at a schoolhouse. I was aware they could have killed us both without a whole lot of effort but chose not to, partly, I'm guessing, because one of us was a woman, and partly because they knew they could kill us later if need be.

I also have no idea what Miss Lyla Case thought we might accomplish once we reached the school. Assuming the people inside were the good guys, Miss Lyla Case and I could hardly be considered desirable reinforcements. An unarmed store clerk and a woman school teacher weren't likely to strike fear into the bad guys, assuming of course, that the men on the outside of the school were the bad guys. I had no opportunity to discuss any of this with Miss Lyla Case as we jounced our way across that piece of prairie ground. Eventually we arrived at the school and I helped Miss Lyla Case get the gelding stopped, which wasn't all that difficult in that he was showing signs of being near the point of collapse.

"We made it," Miss Lyla Case looked at me and nodded a satisfied nod.

"That's true," I said. "We're here all right."

"What do you think we should do now?" she asked me.

The last time she'd asked me that, Miss Lyla Case had ignored my suggestion, so I thought hard this time before answering.

"Best put the horse and buggy around back of the school," I said. "They could shoot him if we leave him here." I nodded in the direction of the gelding who was busy gulping in air and shaking foam off himself.

"I mean, that is if we're planning to stay." I threw that in as an afterthought, although if we'd wanted to leave at that point, we'd have had to do it on foot. I wasn't sure the gelding could make it to the back of the school let alone back over the ground we'd just travelled.

"Of course, we're staying," Miss Lyla Case clucked at the gelding who gathered himself and shuffled around the corner of the school. "We're going to help defend the school."

I was beginning to feel very tired. I wasn't sure if it was from watching that horse twitch and sputter, or if it was from knowing that our situation was not at all good. Or maybe it was the two together.

When we got to the back of the school, Teacher ran around the side of the building. He crouched low to the ground as he came to the wagon.

"What the hell are you doing here?" he said as he took hold the gelding's cheek piece and led us behind the outhouse.

"We came when we saw the shooting," Miss Lyla Case told him.

"Wonderful," Teacher said. "That's just damn wonderful. Well, you can keep on going. Get out of here before you get yourselves killed."

"No." Miss Lyla Case shook her head and stepped down from the buggy. "We're staying."

"Like hell you are," Teacher said.

"We're here to help," said Miss Lyla Case.

"Do you have any guns with you?" Teacher asked.

"Well ... no." Miss Lyla Case shook her head.

"Then it's pretty damned unlikely that you can help."

Teacher had cussed in the presence of a woman four times which was four more times than I'd ever heard him do that before and it looked like he might not be finished cussing just yet. I can't say I blamed him for being unhappy, but I thought I should say something before he set off to using bad language again.

"I don't think we can leave." I nodded in the direction of the horse. "At least not right away."

Teacher seemed to notice the condition of the gelding for the first time.

"Shit," he said.

That made five.

I believe Miss Lyla Case was about to reprimand him for his language when suddenly the shooting started up again. I can tell you very honestly I was quite scared right about then. The sound of guns and bullets was everywhere. Most of the bullets could be heard thudding into the walls of the school or breaking what little glass was left. Some, however, were hitting the outhouse and a few zinged past us overhead.

Teacher said 'come on', or something like that, and led us back into the schoolhouse, all of us in the crouch we'd seen him in before. We got inside the school and immediately saw Virgil Watts, running back and forth behind a barricade built up out of school desks, tables, chairs and textbooks. Every once in a while, he'd pop up at some location in the barricade and snap off a shot from a rifle he was holding.

I'm not much of a firearms expert, so I can't name the rifle Watts was using, but I would say that it was a long way from new. Teacher led us to what looked like a fairly secure spot behind the barricade.

"Sit," he said and pointed in a way that made me want to sit.

Miss Lyla Case must have felt the same way because she said not one word and got down next to me. We had our backs to the firing and for several minutes we didn't speak. The schoolhouse was the kind with windows all along the front (which was behind us as we sat) and a few more windows at the back. The door we came through was now to my right and there was a small cloak room just inside it. That door was the only way in or out. The place had an odd mixture of smells to it — new wood and new paint — both of them mingled with the gunpowder that hung in the air. The shooting got heavier and Miss Lyla Case and I put our heads down and kept them that way for a while. I would have liked to look around but decided to wait until the shooting died back some.

Thing is, it didn't, not for quite some time. We must've sat there with our foreheads pressed against our knees for an hour or better before there was much letup from outside. At one point, Teacher came over and crouched down in front of us.

"This isn't some game," he said. "People are going to die here." He was clearly still unhappy that we were there.

Miss Lyla Case and I both nodded to show that we knew we weren't in a game.

"And there's a pretty fair chance that some of the dying is going to be happening in here," Teacher went on.

I felt that was a bit harsh and maybe unnecessary. I didn't feel he needed to frighten Miss Lyla Case anymore than she already was. Although, as I glanced over at her, I'd have to say she didn't look all that frightened. Nervous maybe, but a long way from terrified.

I'm not sure why but it seemed that Teacher had a sudden change of heart. "We could use your help," he said.

"I told you we came to do just that," Miss Lyla Case looked at Teacher in a way she'd never looked at me. It reminded me my chances with Miss Lyla Case were poorly, at best.

"Yes, Ma'am, I recall your saying that." Teacher smiled for the first time since we'd got there. "It looks like you'll get your opportunity."

He handed Miss Lyla Case his rifle. "Do you know how to use one of these?"

"I'm not an expert shot but yes, I know how to use a rifle."

"Good," Teacher said. "They're spreading out further and further all the time. I wonder if you'd take a spot by a window along this back wall and keep an eye out for anybody trying to come up behind us. Right over there," he pointed, "should be out of the line of fire from the front."

"Of course." Miss Lyla Case was still looking at Teacher the way she had been before. I'd have cut off my leg to have her look at me like that, even once, although I'm embarrassed to admit that those thoughts were in my mind even as all of us were surrounded by men intent, it appeared, on killing us all.

"We made that wall the thickest to keep out the north wind in the winter," Teacher explained. "I don't think they've got anything that will go through, so you should be safe if you stay low. Just be careful when you're looking through the window."

Then he turned to me. He pulled the .44 out of his holster and handed it to me.

"Your job is to watch the door," he said. "If any of them should get by us and come through that door, shoot them. Don't try to be cute and wound somebody in the leg or the arm. You shoot them right smack in the middle, understand?"

"Yes, I do," I said.

To tell the truth I wasn't very happy with the way Teacher had divvied up the responsibilities ... or the guns. I suppose it could be argued that mine was an important job — the door was on the side of the school and I supposed there was a chance that someone could get by our defenses and try to burst in that way. And I was, after all, holding the .44 I had admired for so long. But it still bothered me a little that Miss Lyla Case had the whole back of the school to guard and with a rifle, while I was sitting cross-legged on the floor looking at a door that probably wasn't going to open with a gun I'd probably never shoot.

"Could you tell us what is going on?" Miss Lyla Case asked.

"Some people are shooting at us," Teacher said.

"I am aware of that fact," Miss Lyla Case said. "You needn't condescend."

"I wasn't finished, Ma'am," Teacher went on. "They'd like Watts and me ... me, in particular, to be dead. They've been using the school as an excuse to get at me."

"Who is 'they'?" asked Miss Lyla Case.

For some reason, Teacher didn't answer that question, at least not right away.

When he did speak, "Some men killed a man named Matt Slater about two years ago now," is what he said.

The shooting picked up again and we all got down close to the floor. All except Watts who resumed the running around and shooting from here and there strategy we'd seen earlier.

"Why is he doing that?" I yelled over the noise of the guns.

"We're trying to make them think there's more of us in here than there really is," Teacher was loading shells into another rifle as he spoke.

"Why don't you let us do some shooting then?" I asked. It seemed to me an odd contradiction that two people were trying to make it seem that there were a bunch of people in the school, but that two people who actually were there, were in charge of watching a door and a field and weren't doing any shooting.

I have to say something at this point. I am writing this book because the man we called Teacher was one of the bravest and finest people I have ever met. I liked him better than I'd ever liked anyone in my life, except for my mother and father. I learned from him and admired him. But he was not, Teacher wasn't, real good with strategy. If you've read the part of this that Cal Chapin wrote, you may have already suspected that. Now it doesn't change how I felt about him one little bit, but it's true. Teacher was a fine soldier but not a great general.

Anyway, he didn't answer my question. He left us and went back to the barricade to help Watts. Miss Lyla Case edged over to the windows to keep an eye on the piece of pasture that stretched out behind the school. And I watched the door. Here I was in my first (and it turns out, my last) gun battle and I was ... well, I was mostly bored.

Eventually the firing died down again. It was getting on toward dusk and the light was fading quickly. Teacher crouched down and snuck back over to us.

"We'll try to get you out after dark," he said.

"No need to give that much thought." Miss Lyla Case set her mouth in a firm line. "We're not leaving."

"I appreciate the help, I really do, but ..."

"Look," Miss Lyla Case left the window and crouched down next to me and across from Teacher, "This school is as much mine as it is yours. More, as a matter of fact. I want to help protect it. I'm staying."

"I told you this isn't about the school," Teacher said.

"Yes, you did say that." Miss Lyla Case nodded. "And that's about all you said. You mentioned Matt Slater, was it? I think the least you could do is explain all this."

"I wasn't planning to tell you this," Teacher rubbed his jaw with the butt end of another rifle, "but I wasn't planning on having you drop in either."

He seemed to be deciding whether or not to share that story with us. He nodded and that seemed to indicate he'd made up his mind.

"Matt Slater was my brother." Teacher looked at us as he was talking. "I'd intended to come up here to find his killers anyway but when the opportunity to impersonate a teacher came along, I thought I might be able to do a little investigating without anybody knowing who I really was. Keymore found out though,

I'm not sure how. Turns out it was Keymore or his men who killed Matt. Either way, Keymore was behind it. When he found out who I was, he decided I'd have to die as well, for his own self-protection. He started making a lot of noise about the school, even burned it down once thinking that when I was eventually gunned down, people could be convinced I was killed protecting the school from unknown criminals or vandals or something of the like."

There was something that was bothering me, and I decided to ask him about it.

"If you knew it was Keymore, why didn't you do something before this? Why didn't you go after him?"

Teacher looked at me and smiled. "It was only when I caught up to Cox and Hillier that I knew for certain Keymore had my brother killed. I'm not bad with firearms but I can't beat ten men. That's how many are in Keymore's little army now. I'd hoped to get them two or three at a time and eliminate them that way but since I got back from Canada, they've been pretty careful to stay together."

"Why was your brother shot?" Miss Lyla Case asked.

"Matt was a United States Marshall," Teacher said. "He was on some investigation, I don't know exactly what. The government said it was a land fraud case but that's all they'd tell me, and I wasn't able to get that out of Cox while he was dying."

Those were the first details I had heard up to that time of what had taken place in Canada. (Cal and I didn't discuss the hunt for Hillier and Cox until much later.)

"How did this happen?" Miss Lyla Case looked around the interior of the school. "This ... this siege?"

"Watts and I were doing some repair work up on the roof. Saw the dust cloud coming this way. We knew it was several riders. It's no secret that I stay out here. I guess they decided today was the day."

"Couldn't you have gotten away...outrun them?"

Teacher shook his head. "Maybe, but we knew it might come down to this eventually. We've been waiting, Watts and me for some help. I sent messages to a couple of friends of mine thinking that if they came, the odds might be a little better."

Teacher looked at me. "You met one of them that first day I was here."

I thought back to the incident outside the hotel. "The man you called Harry?"

Teacher smiled again. "Harry Longabaugh. He's done a little outlawin' from time to time. But he's the best gun I know and if he was here, we'd have a chance."

"This is so terrible," Miss Lyla Case said. "People shooting at each other and choosing up sides like in a children's game ... to kill each other."

Teacher nodded. "Like I said before, it's not a game. This is a war ..."

He appeared to have more to say on the subject, but he had to abandon the discussion when the firing began again, worse than it had been at any time so far. They kept it up for quite a while and at one point Miss Lyla Case suddenly raised her rifle and took a shot into the night that was falling all around us.

Teacher ran to her from where he'd been jumping around with Watts.

"Did you see someone?" he shouted over the din of the battle.

"I thought I did," Miss Lyla Case said, "but I'm not sure."

"I can help her," I said. "I'm pretty sure I can look out a window and watch that door over there at the same time."

Teacher looked at me and maybe he understood I wasn't happy with the job I'd been given. Anyway, he nodded, and I went and stood near Miss Lyla Case and looked out at the field behind the school.

"Where was he?" I asked.

"Over there." She pointed.

It was dark but there was a tree standing in the shadows by the corner of the building. I didn't see anyone.

Miss Lyla Case looked at me. I could see she still wasn't scared. At least not like I'd have expected someone like her to be. By that I mean a woman. Which I knew then, and know now, was a wrong way of thinking. Anyway, she wasn't scared. Not like I was. I guess that surprised me a little. I stayed there beside her, and we looked out into the night for a long time. We didn't see anything else and eventually, Miss Lyla Case shrugged and set the rifle down.

"I guess it was nothing," she said. "I'm sorry."

"That's easy enough to do," I told her gently. "If you want to rest for a while, I can watch out here."

She nodded and sat down with her back against the barricades. She closed her eyes and just as she did that the shooting got still worse. There was a yell behind me, and Watts went crashing up against the far wall of the school, blood pumping out of his chest and turning the floor red.

He slid down the wall to the floor and I was sure he was either dead or soon would be, but Teacher and Miss Lyla Case ran to him and started doing things — doctor things — that I didn't understand. Teacher threw me his rifle.

"Here," he yelled over the gunfire. "Do as much shooting as you can but don't get yourself killed."

"Okay," I said.

I snuck a peak up over the barricade and it scared me about to death. There were bullets flying everywhere and it was obvious from what happened to Watts that the barricade was a long way from perfect in the protection end of things.

I decided my best strategy would be to jump up, get off a quick shot and get down again, the way I'd seen Watts and Teacher doing it. I tried it but I sort of slipped as I was pulling the trigger and my first shot went into the sky, a couple of hundred feet over the flashes that showed where Keymore's men were spread out against the horizon.

I looked over at Teacher to see if he'd been watching but he was bent over Watts pressing on his chest, I guessed to stop the bleeding. Miss Lyla Case was tearing a piece off the bottom part of her dress. It had been a pretty dress too. Watts's eyes were open, but I couldn't tell how he was. I figured he must be alive at least or they wouldn't have been bothering with bandaging his wound.

I moved down the barricade a ways, and got off another shot. This one was at least in the general direction and roughly the right height of the people who were shooting at us, but I was in too much of a hurry to get my head back down to spend a lot of time worrying about accuracy. The funny thing is, right after that the shooting died out completely and didn't start up again for the rest of the night. I doubt very much if it was my two stray bullets that discouraged Keymore's riders. More likely they decided to get some sleep and start up again the next day.

I dashed back and forth, here and there on the barricade for a while, not because I wanted to, but because it seemed to be the accepted way of doing things. But I got tired of it after a while and figured since I wasn't actually doing any shooting, I might as well save my breath. I sat down with my back to the barricade, but I no sooner got comfortable than Teacher looked up at me.

"Keep watching out there," he said. "I don't want those birds riding in here while we're having a siesta." I thought about telling him that I wasn't planning to sleep, just rest for a few minutes, but then I thought better of it and found a spot I could see from fairly well. Trouble was, there was nothing to see but black night for a long time. It had clouded over so there were no stars and no moonlight.

I don't know how long I stayed in that position — it wasn't very comfortable I can tell you — before I saw anything I could actually report on. What I finally saw was a fire, a campfire, I guessed, then another, and another until the schoolhouse was pretty much surrounded by those campfires.

"Teacher," I said real quiet.

"Yeah?"

"You might want to take a look here."

He came and looked, then went to the back of the school and looked there too.

"There's about a dozen fires which means they've brought in more men. There'll be at least one man at every fire."

"Why bother with the fires?" I asked him. "It's not all that cold."

"Probably they're just to let us know that getting out of here is pretty much impossible."

I could see that, and I nodded to let him know.

"That's going to make your job that much tougher," Teacher looked at me.

They'd made the fires large, the way an Indian friend of mine said white men usually build fires, and there was enough light from them to create a strange glow inside the schoolhouse. I could see Teacher's face clearly in that light. I had a feeling that what I was about to hear wasn't going to be good news.

"What job is that?"

We need help," he said. "Even if the people I sent for get here, it'll be too late. Watts needs a doctor and we have to have food and water. I want you to go to town."

He said it like what he was asking was for me to ride into town on a peaceful Sunday afternoon, pick up a few sweets and a ham bone for the dog and come on back in time for supper.

"How were you thinking I was to do that?" I asked him. "Go to town, I mean. "

"You'll have to sneak out of here tonight on that horse you brought."

"That horse could be dead, either from a heart attack or one of those bullets that have been flying around and even if he isn't, I don't know if he's broke to ride." After I said that, I had a thought. "Where are your horses?" I asked. "Yours and Watts's."

"They were run off not long after we holed up here," Teacher said. "But there may be some good in that. If you can get through those fires on that buggy horse and ride due east about a mile, there's a watering hole. Watts is sure that Prince will have gone there, and he'll stay there until Watts or somebody else comes for him."

"That's good news?" I was having trouble being as pleased as Teacher was about me riding straight at those fires and the armed men around them on an exhausted buggy horse and if I lived through that, having the opportunity to ride the craziest mustang that ever lived, to town and back.

"That's it." Teacher half smiled, half grinned at me. Even in all this he could see an amusing side to things.

"When you get to town, get anyone who'll pick up a gun to come and help. If there's enough of them, maybe these guys will just ride off. I can't see them wanting a war with the whole town, just to get me."

I nodded but I was still thinking more about the *getting* to town part than I was about what I'd do once I got there.

"And bring food and water," Teacher reminded me. "And the Doctor if he'll come. If not, bring medicine and bandages."

I was beginning to think I'd need a wagon for all the supplies. And I had strong doubts about the possibility of Keymore's men letting me drive up to the school a second time at the reins of a wagon. Not that any of that mattered since I was dead sure I'd never get past the ring of fires and gunmen that had the school surrounded in the first place.

"What about Miss Lyla Case?"

"I talked to her." Teacher looked over at where Miss Lyla Case was sitting on the floor next to Watts. She was leaning against the wall and her eyes were closed but I couldn't tell if she was sleeping or not. Her hair wasn't neat and pretty the way I'd always seen it and her dress was torn and had blood on it, but I don't think I'd ever seen her, or anyone I guess, look as beautiful as she did just then.

"She won't leave," Teacher told me. "Besides, we only have one horse and even if we had two and she was a good rider, we couldn't risk having her try to get through what's out there. And I need her here."

He was looking at her again when he said the part about needing her. I suddenly felt about as tired as I've ever been. I knew there wasn't a lot more to be said.

"When were you thinking I should go?"

"Just before dawn. That's when they're most likely to be asleep. In the meantime, why don't you rest for a while. I'll keep watch."

I handed him the rifle and lay down on the floor. It was a pretty warm night, but I remember shivering for a long time on that floor. I don't know if I actually slept much, I suppose I must have. Eventually I felt Teacher's hand shaking me awake.

"Time to go," he said softly.

I stood up and looked out. The fires had died back some which I took for a good sign. Maybe the reason the fires weren't built up was that the men beside them were sleeping.

'Take the .44 with you," Teacher told me.

"Yeah," I said and that was all the talk that was exchanged between us as I got ready to ride out and get filled with more holes than a prairie dog town.

I was hungry but we'd long since eaten the food Miss Lyla Case and I had planned to have for our picnic. Watts had eaten more than anybody and I was thinking that it would be an awful waste of food the rest of us could have had, if he went ahead and died. I know that was more wrong thinking on my part, but I was mighty unhappy about having to go out and get myself killed and all, so I guess maybe explains why I was in something of a bad mood.

I nodded toward Miss Lyla Case and Watts but, in what was left of the light from the fires, I could see they were both asleep. Then I stepped outside. I'll admit it plain; I've never been more scared in my life before or since. It was probably five minutes before I took my first step away from the door of the schoolhouse and that step was a small one. The clouds had drifted off and the moon was out, which although it probably didn't make things any brighter than they were already, what with all the bonfires, still made me feel a good deal worse. The one thing that cheered me up a little, not much mind you, was the fact that the gelding was standing in the lee of the outhouse, which meant he was in shadow. I figured I'd at least be able to get mounted before I got shot. To tell the truth, there was a part of me wishing that horse had died during the night. That way I'd at least get to die inside the schoolhouse in the company of friends and the most beautiful woman, I or Kecking Horse, had ever seen, instead of on the prairie where carrion eaters would be the only ones to even take notice.

Eventually I knew I had to move. I got down on my belly and kind of skittered along the ground in the direction of the outhouse. The gelding nickered. He probably figured I was bringing him something to eat. His head was down, and he looked like he hadn't moved more than a few feet from where I'd left him. Which may explain why Keymore's men hadn't run him off like they had the others. They likely thought the horse was dying. He sure looked like he was dying. I wasn't at all confident that, if by some miracle we survived the ride through the fires, this animal would get me to the watering hole where Teacher was so certain Prince would be waiting.

I got to the gelding, rose to my knees and reached up and patted him on the neck. He turned his head a couple of degrees at the most, quite a bit less than a quarter turn, and blinked.

"Easy, old boy," I whispered to him. "I'm just going to climb aboard, and we'll ride on out of here."

He blinked again.

"I know it sounds a touch far-fetched, but it can be done," I said, not believing for one minute that it could be done at all. Not likely on a fleet-footed thoroughbred, and sure as hell not on this horse.

I started pulling the harness off him, there hadn't been time to do that before, and I'll say one thing for working with a horse that's close to death — there isn't a whole lot of fidgeting and fussing goes on. The whole time I was undoing clips and pulling off harness, I was trying to decide on my best strategy — whether to try to sneak past Keymore's men or to bolt through them, the idea there being that I might be by them before they could react. I had the harness off the gelding and rigged up a set of reins and a bridle and still hadn't decided on which strategy to try.

I knew I didn't have any more time to think about it, so I decided to use a little piece of each tactic. My plan was to sneak up real slow and get as close as I dared to the fires, then give the gelding the dickens and we'd go to beat blazes. It wasn't much of a scheme, I knew that, but it was about all I could come up with. It might have worked too if that carriage horse had been as good at going to beat blazes as he was at sneaking up real slow.

I got up on him and we worked our way up pretty close to what I figured were the two smallest fires. Then I took a piece of rawhide and gave him one good lick on his hind quarters and yelled 'yaah' as loud as I've ever yelled anything in my life.

Nothing happened. The gelding didn't burst forward, he didn't lunge, jump, buck or flinch.

He didn't even sneak. In fact, if I recall correctly, and you must remember this all happened some time ago, that horse took a step backward.

I immediately realized that hollering 'yaah' had been a serious mistake. Based on all the noise and commotion that followed, I judged that most of Keymore's men had been asleep when I yelled. And none of them were now. I kicked and whipped the gelding until my legs and arm hurt. Nothing.

Now I'm not a religious person. I guess I'm more like my pa in that respect than Mother who has spent a great deal of time trying to convert first Pa, then me and most recently, Nettie Whitman. But I want you to know that after that night in the field out by the schoolhouse, I do believe in miracles. Because what happened just then was a miracle, no argument about it.

As you can appreciate, once the men at the fires got themselves sorted out, there was a considerable amount of shooting going on. Fortunately, not all of it was directed at me. Some of the men, who were either too far away to see me or were a little slow-witted when roused suddenly from sleep, started shooting at the school. Teacher, I guessed it was him, returned some of their fire. About the only person who wasn't blasting away at something was me. With all the excitement, I never actually got around to taking Teacher's .44 out of my belt.

Still, there was no mistaking the fact that a good portion of the firing was coming in my direction. I figured I had minutes, maybe only seconds to live, particularly as none of the shooting had apparently been able to provide the gelding with sufficient reason to move. I was doing quite a bit of yelling by that time but because all of it was drowned out by the noise of the gunfire and also because I'm not real proud of the things I was yelling — a lot of the words were ones I didn't know I knew — I'll not repeat them here.

That's when the miracle I referred to took place. A bullet grazed the gelding's backside — I checked later, it was a little up and to the left of his tail. Suddenly the horse that I was certain had no run left in him, lit out like his hind end was on fire, which may very well be what he thought was happening.

Now I've ridden a lot of fast horses in my life, but this was the first horse I'd ever ridden one that had a bullet crease its rear. I recommend it for those who require their horses to move out quickly. What's bad about it is, that steering a horse that has gone through this particular experience is pretty much impossible. The result was the gelding and I, instead of going between fires, the way I'd planned it out, were headed straight at one. The fire the gelding chose to run at had two of Keymore's men, one on each side of it, shooting at us as fast as they could reload and fire.

I figured, sure as sin, the gelding would go right at that fire, stop dead and I'd get thrown over his head and directly into the flames. That way I could get shot and burned to a crisp all at the same time.

But I had misjudged the gelding at that particular moment of his life. He didn't stop. He *did not* stop and that's a fact. He ran right through that fire — never slowed down so much as a tick.

I think the men who were doing the shooting found this to be kind of strange behaviour for a horse. Which is maybe why they stopped shooting. In fact, it was as if all of Keymore's men stopped shooting. It certainly seemed quiet all of a sudden. As that carriage horse raced through and beyond the fires and still there were no sounds of bullets following us along, I guess I got into the spirit of the moment (for different reasons than the gelding, I admit), and once more I yelled 'yaah!'

Chapter Thirteen

While the bullet hitting the horse where it did, and when it did, was a blessing as far as getting us past Keymore's men was concerned, it brought me face to face with another problem. A horse that wasn't going to let a bonfire make him whoa wasn't about to listen to the suggestions of the man on his back. In other words, turning the gelding in the direction of the waterhole or any other direction than the one we were going in was out of the question. I hauled on that right rein as hard as I knew how — even used two hands — but that carriage horse kept going in a line so true you could have used it for a straight edge.

Eventually my arms wore out and I decided to wait until either the damn gelding died of a heart attack or we reached Denver. I'm not sure how much ground we covered, the horse running as hard as he could, me trying to stay on which was getting more difficult because it had started to rain, and his back was getting pretty slippery. I also spent a fair amount of time looking back to see if any of Keymore's men were in pursuit. It appeared they had decided a man on a loco horse running away from the school, (and also away from the town), wasn't worth chasing. I didn't see or hear any sign of them.

Finally, that horse began to tire and, although it probably took the better part of a mile to complete the job, I finally got him turned roughly in a line with where I figured the watering hole ought to be. It was about that time the gelding must've realized he was plumb exhausted. So, our rate of speed going in the direction I wanted to go was about a quarter what it had been when we were going where *he* wanted to go.

As a result, it was a good long time before we got to the watering hole. We probably would have missed it entirely except we got close enough for the gelding to smell the water and he took us the last stretch pretty much on his own. By the time we reached the place — it wasn't much, just a small slough between a bunch of poplars — it was raining so hard that even though dawn was well on its way to breaking, I couldn't see the trees until I was almost in them. The good thing was the horses found each other, which meant I didn't have to spend a lot of time tramping around in the mud looking for Prince.

I wasn't looking forward to dealing with him after what I'd seen in that pasture a few weeks before, but I knew the carriage horse wasn't an option. Even if he'd been able to keep moving, he wasn't about to leave that water or those other horses. I briefly considered waiting for the rain to stop but then I thought about Miss Lyla Case in that schoolhouse and Watts likely to die from his wound and I knew I'd have to catch Prince and get moving as quick as I could.

The horses were occupied with sniffing noses, squealing and other horse to horse stuff so, surprised as all get out, I was able to get the bridle and rigged up reins off of the gelding's head and onto Prince with almost no fuss. But even at that, I can't say I was looking forward to the ride to town on Watts' mustang. I figured he might be one of those horses that would be decent for one man and a pig for another. Especially one that didn't even have a saddle.

I was wrong about that. Prince wasn't a pig at all. I don't know if he had some sense that Watts needed help or what, but I got on him and we rode off like old friends. He wasn't real excited about the rain but once we got out of those trees and were pointed more or less in the direction of town, he became real agreeable.

The carriage horse, stupid as ever, followed us. All the time I'd spent trying to make that fool gelding go where I wanted, and all Prince had to do was nicker and trot off. The gelding ambled after us like it was his plan all along.

The rain didn't let up, but it didn't matter much. I was already too wet to care anymore so we splashed along until we got to the road, then angled for town. I kicked Prince into a lope which he didn't like much. Some horses don't much care for water splashing up high on their legs and their bellies and I figured maybe Prince was of such a mind. All the same, although he threw his head some and swished his tail, he kept moving along until at last I saw a few lights and finally the clapboard buildings of Kecking Horse.

We turned into the main street and for the first time I realized I had no idea what I was going to do. I'd been so occupied with just *getting to* town, I admit I hadn't given any thought at all to what I'd do when I got there. And even though Teacher told me *what* he wanted done, he hadn't offered many ideas as to how I was to accomplish the necessary tasks.

With the morning growing lighter, I got Prince stopped under the overhang from the National Land and Grain building, and as we stood there out of the rain, I put together my plan. I needed three things: people (not just anybody but people who could, and would, use guns), food and water and, of course, a doctor for Watts. I decided to leave the supplies to the last. I'd start by putting together the people who would ride out there with me to stand up to Keymore's men.

Now I could fill the next dozen pages or so with the excuses I heard from the people I talked to, but I don't want to do that. I do want you to know that I've never been more disgusted in my life with the people I'd grown up with as friends and neighbours. Of course, there were some people I knew better than to ask — Jake Drury, for example and Cooper Raine.

Of those I did try to recruit, which included everyone from Archie Cuddy to Mr. Westover, and even Mr. Marcus Warren, only two said they'd come with me. Those two were Floyd Martel, the implement man who played such great fiddle at the dance and Toots Parenteau. To be honest, I wasn't sure either one of them would turn out to be particularly handy with a gun. Both of them *had* guns, at least, although Floyd's wasn't much more than a squirrel rifle and Toots' weapon looked old enough to have seen service at the Little Bighorn. There was one other man I knew would have joined us; that was Cal Chapin, but Cal was away for a few days and no one was sure exactly where he'd gone.

Doc Fenster was one of those who refused to go — his excuse was a little more acceptable than most I'd heard — the town needed its doctor alive and healthy in order to keep others the same way. What I didn't like was how he said "it looks like I'm going to be a very busy man shortly." He was right, it turned out, though not near as busy as Archie Cuddie who handled the town's undertaking requirements, but I didn't like the doctor saying that with what appeared to me to be a certain amount of anticipation. He did give us some bandages and other stuff he thought would help with Watts's wound.

Toots and I gathered up some supplies. The town's ladies sent a lot of baking, I think some of them were embarrassed their men turned out cowardly, and I tied a barrel of water on a pack horse. Then I changed into some dry clothes, saddled Powder, my own horse, and we were ready to ride. I'd only been in town maybe three hours at the most. The last thing I did before we left was ask around one last time to see if Teacher's friend, that Harry Longabaugh fella, had showed up yet. I had a feeling he might've evened up the odds quite a bit out there at the schoolhouse. But nobody'd seen him and there was nothing left but to ride back out there, the three of us.

The one good thing was it had quit raining and although the day was grey and foul with an icy feeling north wind, at least we'd be dry. Turns out I was a little mistaken about that too because we travelled at a high lope most of the way which made for a fair amount of splashing mud and after a while, we were all pretty much covered.

We reined up about a half or three quarters of a mile from the school on that same rise Miss Lyla Case and I had first looked down and seen all the shooting. The fires were out — no need for them in daylight I guessed and, of course, it would have been difficult to keep them going through the rain. J. Emerson Keymore's men were still spread out but weren't completely surrounding the school so I figured we'd at least be able to get down there through the gap between them.

Thinking back on it now, I suppose Keymore really only wanted Teacher and Watts. Maybe he thought killing townspeople would get him into trouble, even in a town populated mostly by cowards (of course, he wouldn't have known that part). Anyway, that would explain why we were allowed to ride in there pretty much without any trouble, just as Miss Lyla Case and I had done earlier. What did happen was J. Emerson Keymore rode over to us as we were circling around toward the back of the school. He approached with his right hand up and away from his gun to show he wasn't hostile, but I noticed Floyd Martel kept that squirrel gun aimed right at him, just in case. It seemed strange to me but Keymore had a black suit on, more like he was going off to church than trying to kill some people.

"I've no quarrel with any of you," Keymore said.

We all looked at him, but I guess none of the three of us could think of anything to say so we just sat there quiet except for the sound of horses breathing and snorting. Mr. Keymore waited for quite a while for somebody to say something but when nobody did, I reckon he figured he should say some more.

"If you go down there and join up with those two men, there's a good chance you'll be killed," he said. "I don't want it that way, but I also want you to know we will get the men we're after no matter what it takes or who gets hurt."

"There's a woman in that schoolhouse," Floyd said.

Keymore nodded. "Yes, and that's very unfortunate, very unfortunate indeed. When you get to the school, tell her that is she leaves now, we won't do anything to stop her or harm her. You have my word on that."

"She won't leave," I said.

"Then there's nothing I can do." Keymore shook his head and I suppose he was trying to look solemn but if that's what he was doing, it wasn't very convincing. At least I wasn't convinced.

We didn't say anything to that, and another long silence followed while Keymore looked at us one at a time and we all looked back at him.

"I'm willing to let you ride down, get the woman, and ride back out. The four of you." He looked at his watch. "I'll give you until noon. After that there'll be no chance for any of you."

I looked over at Toots and Floyd. Toots was smiling and Floyd spat some chew. It passed awful close to Keymore's boot on its way to the ground. I didn't figure I needed to add anything, so I just sat.

"The man in that school is a killer, plain and simple," Keymore pointed at the schoolhouse, "and you should think very carefully about which side you choose to throw in with."

"That ain't exactly the cream of society you got out there with you," Floyd said. I hadn't realized Floyd was as feisty as he was. There was no coward in him; that was certain.

J. Emerson Keymore looked like he was beginning to lose patience with us, but he didn't answer Floyd. Instead he looked at me.

"What about you? You got anything to say?"

"You killed Teacher's brother," I said. "United States Marshall Matt Slater, you killed him, or had him killed."

Of course, I didn't realize my saying that pretty well doomed the three of us, or maybe I wouldn't have said it. Mr. Keymore appeared not to appreciate having people in the community being aware of what had happened with Matt Slater, and he let us know that. He pointed first at me, then at each of the other two and then back at me.

"You're dead," he said. "All three of you are dead."

Then he turned and rode back to his men. Toots, Floyd, and me continued on down to the school. We went along at a fast trot.

Floyd said, "We aren't loping our horses. I'm damned if I'll run from that son of a bitch." Like I said, this was a side of Floyd I hadn't seen before.

I think all three of us knew that Keymore's men could have gunned us down in a matter of a few seconds but none of us kicked our horses into a lope. And there were no shots fired. Maybe Keymore was holding to his noon deadline.

We rode directly in behind the and tied our horses as close to the schoolhouse as we could, hoping that maybe that would keep Keymore's men from running them off. We unloaded the supplies and water and hustled inside. We no sooner got inside than there was a hail of gunfire at the schoolhouse and we all lay on the floor for a while, the newcomers and those who were already there nodding greetings to one another. Apparently, the offer to leave in safety was off the table.

The shooting didn't last long that time, and in a few minutes, we were able to stand up and brush ourselves off. Teacher looked at me, then at Toots and finally at Floyd.

"Harry Longabaugh didn't make it," I explained.

"I see that," Teacher said. Then he smiled. "Thank you both for coming." He shook hands with Toots and Floyd.

I looked around the schoolhouse. Watts was lying pretty well where he'd been when I'd left the night before (actually it seemed like a week had passed since Teacher tapped me and said it was time to go). Miss Lyla Case was sitting at the windows watching the back of the school yard like she had before. But I noticed a difference in her, actually a few differences. The first was her clothes. The dress was gone. It had been replaced by a man's shirt and a pair of men's pants. I recognized them as Teacher's. Her hair was pulled back and tied up at the back. Her bare feet were resting on part of a desk that sat in front of her. But the biggest change was in her face, especially about the eyes. The woman who was guarding the back of the school was very different from the woman who'd grabbed onto me when the gelding had bolted down the road during our buggy ride.

"Miss Lyla Case," I touched my hat to her, "I believe you know Floyd Martel and Toots Parenteau."

She nodded at the three of us. As I watched her, I knew she was prepared to die in the fight for that school. Except it wasn't the school she'd be dying for; I knew that too.

"I brought some things I figured we'd need." I opened the bundle with the food and the stuff Doc Fenster had sent. Teacher took the medicine and bandages and went over to Watts. He bent down and pulled back the makeshift bandages to clean the wound. To me it looked quite a bit worse.

"I'm pretty handy doctorin' animals and such," Floyd Martel said, and he knelt down to help Teacher.

Teacher looked up at Toots. "If you wouldn't mind keeping an eye on things out front," he pointed to a part of the barricade that looked like it had been reinforced during the night. It appeared to me Teacher had given up on his idea of making Keymore think there were more people in the schoolhouse. From my conversation with Keymore on the way in, I figured that was a good decision. Keymore knew exactly how many people were in the schoolhouse. Maybe the only thing he didn't know was that Watts was shot up bad.

The place Teacher directed Toots to looked fairly safe. I was hoping I wouldn't be given the job of watching the door again. But Teacher didn't tell me to do that or anything else for that matter. I wondered if he was angry I'd only brought two men back with me.

I asked Miss Lyla Case if she'd like something to eat and she nodded that she would. I made her up a sandwich and poured out a glass of water and took them over to her. She looked at me and smiled a little bit. She looked more tired than I'd seen anybody look in a long time.

"Miss Lyla Case, if you'd like to rest, I can watch here for a while," I said.

"Thank you." She nodded and got down from where she was and I took over.

There isn't a lot to tell about that day. It got very hot for that time of year and by the middle of the afternoon I was wishing it would cloud over or the wind would blow or something to cool things, but none of that happened and about all we did most of the day was sit in sweat and keep watch.

In the hottest part of the afternoon Watts started raving, went delirious Teacher said. He was yelling a lot of stuff which didn't make any sense but every once in a while you'd hear him holler something about horses and once, clear as day, he yelled out, "Prince, you son of a bitch." Not long after that he went back to sleep, a quiet sleep, but to be honest, when I looked at him, I figured the man was dying. I was hoping he wouldn't so I could tell him that Prince wasn't a son of a bitch after all. I expect he knew that anyway when he wasn't sick and delirious.

The day passed without any more shooting from outside; in fact, it didn't look like much of anything was happening out there. Along toward sundown it finally began to cool off. Toots got down from where he'd been watching the front of the school and Floyd took his spot. Toots said he'd whip us up a little dinner. Did pretty good too, of course, it was cold, he didn't have anything to cook with or anything, but it was a meal I won't probably ever forget. While Toots was preparing the food, ham and a potato salad and some other things, Teacher came over and said he'd spell me at my spot.

"What do you think is going to happen?" I asked him.

"I don't know for sure, he said, "but my guess is we won't have to wait much longer to find out."

I nodded and got down to let him take over and I saw he was holding out his hand to me. I wasn't sure what it was about, but I shook his hand anyway.

"That was a hell of a thing you did," he said. "Thanks."

"I wish I could have got more men to ... or the doctor ..."

He shook his head I guess to tell me I didn't have to explain.

"You better get some food and rest up some," he said. "I don't think we'll be getting a lot of sleep tonight."

It was then that I noticed dried blood all over his left wrist and hand. I pointed at it.

"You get hit?"

He nodded. "Ricochet shot, I think. Bad luck." Then he grinned. "The good thing is I'm right-handed."

"Yeah," I said. "Guess so."

I got down and took on a pretty good helpin of Toots' supper. While I ate, I thought about all the possibilities for how the thing we were in was going to end. I quit that after a while though because every way I thought about it, the end turned out bad.

Looking back on it after, I came to the conclusion that J. Emerson Keymore's strategy was to hit us when we were most tired. If that was his plan, it was a good one. During the night, I expect Keymore's men slept, except for a couple maybe, who kept an eye on the school in case we tried another run for town. Inside the schoolhouse nobody slept, except Watts and I wouldn't call what he was doing sleeping, at least not the restful kind. The others of us were edgy, waiting for the sneak attack we were sure would come.

When it finally did come, we were exhausted from staring out into the night. It finally did cloud over and the moonless, starless night — Keymore built no fires this night — made us work still harder at trying to spot any movement in that dark that was like the inside of a cave.

They rushed us just before dawn. Miss Lyla Case and Floyd were at the back wall, Teacher and Toots were watching the front and I was sitting on the floor trying to give Watts a drink of water. He was full of fever and pretty well unconscious, so I wasn't getting more than a few drops into him.

When the shooting started, I thought at first it was just another barrage of far off gunfire, like all the other times. It wasn't long before I knew, all of us knew, that this time was different. For one thing, they were closer. I don't know if Toots and Teacher had fallen asleep or just couldn't spot them coming, but suddenly Keymore's men were all around the school, shooting and throwing sticks with burning straw tied to them at the building.

Toots was hit almost right away, and he yelled loud enough for Keymore's men to know they'd got one of us. I had just taken the .44 out of my belt when the side door crashed open and two men were in the room throwing bullets everywhere. I shot the first one who came through the door. I found out later the man I shot was named Dirty Jim James. My bullet hit him smack in the middle of the chest and my guess is he was dead before he hit the floor. I hope he was.

The second man in — his name was Korn — was loading and firing as fast as most people could shoot a pistol. Floyd Martel jumped out to line up a shot at him, but Korn cut him down before Floyd could pull the trigger. Miss Lyla Case turned and killed Korn with a blast from a shotgun. I didn't even know she had a shotgun, I guess it was one of the things I hadn't noticed, but she had one all right (probably Watts's when I think about it) and she used it to blow Virgil Korn apart, right there at the door of the schoolhouse.

I heard someone outside yell 'let's go' and there was the sound of a lot of horses running away from the school. I looked around and saw Teacher at the top of the barricade firing out into the night. Miss Lyla Case was holding up Floyd Martel who had fallen against her when he was shot. Toots was lying face down on the floor at the far end of the schoolhouse.

Things looked bad. The only good thing that happened was the fires Keymore's men tried to start hadn't amounted to much. I stamped out one as I ran to where Toots was lying. When I rolled him over, I knew right away he was dying. I don't know how I knew that. I'm no medical man, that's for sure, but there was something in his face, in his eyes; something was fading out of him even as I crooked his head under my arm. He never spoke, couldn't, I guess, but he kept looking at me. It seemed like a long time although it probably wasn't a minute and then he just stopped breathing.

I didn't move for quite a while even after Toots died. Teacher knelt down beside me and put his hand on my shoulder.

"You can lay him down now. It's okay."

And I set Toots back down on the floor that was wet and dark with his blood.

Floyd's wounds weren't all that bad. He'd been hit twice, once high up on the right shoulder and the other just a graze below his left hip. Miss Lyla Case was already working on patching him up. It looked like after the first shock wore off, he'd be okay.

Teacher and I went over to where the two men who'd come through the door were lying. One had fallen on the other and as the first light of day filtered into the schoolhouse, I could see their faces twisted in death and their blood running together onto the floor. Teacher opened the door and heaved first one, then the other out onto the ground outside. I guess he did that just to spare us having to look at them. Or maybe it was a message to Keymore, I don't know for sure. He closed the door and took one of the blankets that was covering Watts and went over and laid it over Toots Parenteau.

"They took our horses," Miss Lyla Case said. She was at the back wall looking outside.

The four of us who could still stand looked at each other for a time. Teacher had a smile on his face, but it wasn't a smile that spoke of humour or anything pleasant. I guess right then he knew, as we all did, there was no way we could win this fight, or even escape from the school. And we also knew help wouldn't get there in time to do much for us, if it came at all.

I guess, thinking back on it now, Teacher's smile was kind of a sad thing. I don't say I ever knew the man that well, certainly not as well as I would have liked to, but I knew him well enough to feel certain he didn't want to die. Especially just then when there were some things in his life he didn't want to let go of.

"I'll need my gun," he said to me.

I handed him the .44.

"What are you going to do?" Miss Lyla Case asked.

Teacher waited some before he answered, like he was looking for the right words to say.

"I think maybe if I can get Keymore, the rest of them will quit the fight," he said. "It's mostly between him and me anyway. I don't think those other men are thinking about much more than a pay check. If I can eliminate the man who signs the check, the rest of them might just ride off."

"How do you plan to do that?" Miss Lyla Case was looking hard at him.

"I think I can surprise them," Teacher told her.

It's strange or maybe it's just human nature but even as Teacher was telling us what he was going to do, there was a part of me that was saying — that's not a bad plan, it might work — I guess I didn't want to admit the obvious.

Miss Lyla Case admitted it. "That's suicide," she said. "If you go out there you'll die before you even get close to Keymore."

"Maybe not," Teacher was smiling that same smile again, the one I suppose had more to do with the word inevitable than anything else. "Besides I can't think of a better idea. We have one man dead, two wounded, one badly, and the four of us won't hold them off if they attack again. And they will. But first they'll wait us out until we're starving and exhausted. And it won't be much of a fight then."

I noticed Teacher didn't include himself in the count of the wounded. I looked at Miss Lyla Case. I could see she was trying to think of another argument.

"I'll go with you," Floyd said.

"No, you won't," Teacher told him. "And if you ... if any of you," he looked at me and even at Miss Lyla Case as he was saying it, "step out that door I'll shoot your legs out from under you."

"Maybe someone will come," I said. "Your friend Harry or ..."

"No," he said. "Not now. They'd have been here already if they were coming."

I didn't believe Teacher would shoot any of us in the legs to keep us from following him. I don't think Miss Lyla Case did either and I suspect Teacher knew we didn't believe it.

"If I don't get Keymore, they'll come for Watts," he said. "You'll have your chance to fight then."

"Tom," Miss Lyla Case said in a voice soft as summer wind.

It was the first time I'd ever heard Teacher's real name. I didn't even know it until that moment. He stepped up to her and put his hand on her face. No kiss or embrace, just his hand against her cheek, but that one touch like that, I knew that he loved her. I turned and walked to the barricade. I figured I'd get ready to do what I could once Teacher went out there. Floyd handed me Toots' rifle and we climbed up to where we could get some shots at Keymore's men even though they were too far away for us to hit anything.

The strange thing is I wasn't ready when it started. I don't know what I thought exactly, but suddenly Teacher was outside and running straight at Keymore and his men. It was a while before they even saw him so not much happened until he'd gone maybe a hundred yards or maybe more. That's when they must have seen him coming. Keymore's men fanned out in a line about thirty or forty yards across. J. Emerson Keymore, easy to spot in his black suit, was just about in the middle. I could see them raising their rifles to take aim but so far there had been no shooting. Not by Teacher. Not by them.

I looked back at the door and Miss Lyla Case was standing just outside, right next to where the two dead men were lying. She was watching Teacher and for a minute I wondered if she might still go after him. But then she seemed to make up her mind and climbed up on the barricade with Jake and me. She just got up there when the shooting started. Keymore's men began firing at Teacher who was still running, hunched over, straight at them. He was out there maybe two hundred yards now and closing on the line of men. As soon as they started shooting, Teacher began returning their fire, using the rifle. The .44 was in his holster. And still he ran.

We let fly with everything we had from the schoolhouse, which wasn't much. Miss Lyla Case had abandoned the shotgun and taken up one of the rifles, Watts's, I think. Floyd had his squirrel gun and I was using Toots' rifle. I probably had the best weapon of the three of us but I'm not much of a shot. So, though we desperately wanted to make things uncomfortable for Keymore's men, I'm not sure accomplished much.

As Teacher got closer to the line of men, the shooting became more intense. I knew it wouldn't be long before people died. There wasn't much distance between them now. One of Keymore's men toppled from his horse, then another and for a brief second, I found myself believing Teacher could somehow do something that seemed so impossible. He had the .44 out and was close enough he was clearly causing problems for the other side. But just as my hopes were beginning to rise — I can't speak for the others in the schoolhouse — they were just as quickly dashed.

Teacher went down. Miss Lyla Case screamed. As soon as Teacher hit the ground, Keymore's men rode ahead, still shooting. We could hear them yelling, like they were cheering. Floyd and I continued to blast away as fast as we could reload. One of the riders grabbed at his arm and then fell from his horse. I don't know which of us fired the shot that hit him. But it didn't slow them. Keymore's men rode to the place where Teacher was on the ground.

He had got to his knees and was shooting again. He fired round after round first from the .44, then when it was empty, from the rifle. We saw his body contort and turn almost sideways as he must have taken another bullet, maybe more than one.

Suddenly the line of riders stopped and as I looked away from Teacher to Keymore's men, I realized J. Emerson Keymore wasn't on his horse. I looked back a ways, and saw him lying, face down and still, in a low part of the ground, still muddy from the rain. Even from the schoolhouse I could see a big red patch on the black suit and though it isn't right, I know I was glad that man was dead. Then the other riders rode on, straight at Teacher, who was bent over, almost to the ground, no longer shooting. Floyd took Miss Lyla Case's arm and turned her away. But I watched. I couldn't turn away. And I saw them form a half circle around Teacher and shoot round after round into him. I thought they would never stop but they did finally.

Without Keymore to lead them and with their main target shot down, the men didn't appear to know what to do next. They sat on their horses for a long time looking at the man most of them had never even met who was lying there on the prairie. Then they slowly rode past him and down to the school.

When they got close, Waincastle, I recognized him, yelled for us to come out.

I looked at Floyd and Miss Lyla Case. She shook her head. "They can come in and get us," she said softly and turned and aimed her rifle at the door. I'm not sure what happened exactly since I'd climbed down from the barricade and was crouched down on the floor. Apparently one of Keymore's men had the idea to burn us out and threw one of those burning straw things in a front window. This one landed on the wooden barricade and quickly flared up. Floyd and I tried to put it out, but we were pretty well out of water and didn't have much else to fight a fire with. It quickly grew and in only a few minutes the far side of the school was in flames. I went over to where Toots Parenteau still lay under the blanket and I sort of manoeuvred him onto my shoulder. I didn't want to leave him in there to burn up. Miss Lyla Case and Floyd half carried, half drug Watts to the door and we stumbled out of the burning schoolhouse, over the bodies of the two dead men and stopped in front of the horses of Keymore's men. None of us had brought our guns.

I looked up and saw there were eight of them. Most of them had their guns out and were pointing them at us. Waincastle cocked his pistol. I think he was planning to shoot Watts, but I'm not sure. One of the other men, a man I didn't know and still don't to this day, moved his horse between Waincastle and us.

"We've done enough here," he said, "I'm not for shooting women and unarmed men."

"I owe that black bastard ..." Waincastle said.

"You owe him nothing," the other man said. "From the look of him, he may die anyway. And if he doesn't, then maybe he's a lucky man. Anything more we do here will get us all hung. Let's ride."

Waincastle didn't move right away and the other man said it again. "We ride ... now."

And slowly, very slowly, they turned their horses and rode just as slowly away. They rode past the place they'd tied our horses, leaving them where they stood. Then they rode past Teacher; not one of them touched his hat or even looked down at him.

And, as we stood next to the burning schoolhouse and watched them go, the event that was to be known as the Kecking Horse School Trouble came to an end.

* * *

There were some things I never did find out. I never learned, for example, why Matt Slater was killed or what the land fraud was he'd been investigating. Teacher never explained that. Maybe he didn't know himself.

And I never found out whether Keymore killed Matt Slater himself or had it done. Not that it matters much, I guess. I'm sure it didn't matter to Teacher. Keymore was to blame and he died for it. The others of his men who died that day were Dirty Jim James and Ruben Korn who died inside the schoolhouse and Suitcase Bill Lambert and Joad Cook in that final shootout with Teacher out on the prairie. Cook, you will recall, was with Marty Waincastle that first night Teacher and Watts arrived in town. Add to them the deaths of Hillier and Cox up in Canada and Nate Gillis, the man Teacher killed the night of the dance and you realize how bloody a thing it all was.

Four years have passed now, and the events of that time aren't talked about as much now except by Cooper Raine, of course, and every time he tells it, his part in it gets bigger. Watts recovered and a few weeks later during the first big snow of the winter, he climbed on Prince and rode north to rejoin his family in Canada. Miss Lyla Case stayed until the end of the school term — the school wound up back in the Ramsay bunkhouse — then she left the area. She wrote once, to say she was a tutor for a wealthy family in Kalispell, and that all was well with her. I hope that's true. There's a new schoolhouse being planned. This one will be built right on the edge of town. Our teacher now is Miss Patricia Morgan, which in itself is an odd coincidence, in that Morgan was the fictitious name Teacher used when he first applied to teach here.

Cal Chapin made several trips back and forth to that ranch he wrote about, the one owned by the Burnside women. One of those times he rode north, he just didn't bother coming back. I saw him a few months back when he came by Kecking Horse to visit and drop off the part of the story he wrote. He said he and Ef had three children — that's one for each year he's been up there — and things were going along just fine. It seems to me Cal smiles more now than he used to, and he looks like a contented man.

Teacher (I still think of him by that name) and Toots Parenteau are buried close to each other and not far from town. I'd rather not say exactly where because there may still be those around who would take pleasure in doing damage to their graves. The only time I ever told someone exactly where Teacher is buried was when Harry Longabaugh and his friend Butch came by to pay their respects. Harry told me he felt bad that he couldn't get here in time to help. I never saw them again after that.

Floyd Martel's shoulder didn't heal quite right and he was never able to play the fiddle again. I think it bothered him a lot. Then last year, Floyd died from some disease Doc Fenster had never seen before and didn't know the name of. I guess there wasn't much he could do.

As I said at the beginning of this, I'm about the only one left to tell the story, which is why I decided to tell it. My life has been pretty good, I'd have to say, since the autumn of '96 and all that happened then. Mr. Westover made me a partner in the store and both our names are on the big sign above the door now. I bought our old ranch, the one my parents owned before Pa was killed. I bought it just after Sarah-Beth and I got married. Between the store and the ranch, even though it's just a small spread, we keep mighty busy. Mother chose to stay in town and moved in with Nettie Whitman. The two of them get along very well which is a great surprise to me. An even bigger surprise is Mother's new found interest in frilly underthings. She doesn't seem to care at all about what people say about her which I suppose is good ... in a way.

That just leaves Sarah-Beth and me here in the ranch house. And our son, of course. He's two years old now. His name is Thomas, I guess that doesn't surprise you at all. Sarah-Beth is expecting again for sometime in the late spring. We still go to all the dances even though we're back to Cooper's mouth organ, Nettie's nose-singing and whining dogs. I don't mind it as much anymore, especially when Sarah-Beth presses up against me, just the way she did at that first dance.

If I look up at the mantle over the fireplace, I can see the three things Doc Fenster gave me from Teacher's belongings. There's the book by Emily Bronte, it's one of my favourites; there's that magnifying glass Teacher said he could set people on fire with (I don't know if that was really true or not) and there's the .44 calibre Smith and Wesson ... Teacher's gun. I don't expect I'll ever fire it again. Don't really want to.

A book, a magnifying glass and a gun. That feels like an odd combination of words to me. But I guess those objects and those words represent a time and a man I'll not forget.

David A. Poulsen has been a broadcaster, teacher, professional cowboy, football coach, stage and film actor and—most of all—writer.

His writing career began in earnest when his story *The Welcomin'* won the 1984 Alberta Culture Short Story Competition.

Now the author of 27 books, many for middle readers and young adults, David spends 60 to 80 days a year in classrooms and libraries across Canada (and beyond) as a visiting author/presenter.

The UBC Creative Writing alumnus and former Writer in Residence at the Saskatoon Public Library recently made his inaugural foray into the world of adult crime fiction with *Serpents Rising*, the best-selling first book in the Cullen and Cobb Mystery series. There are now four titles in the series and the fourth—*None So Deadly*—hit bookstores in the spring of 2019. *The Man Called Teacher* is his first adult western.

David lives on a small ranch in Alberta's foothills where he and his wife Barb raise and train running-bred quarter horses for barrel racing competitions.